MARKED IMMORTALS

DARK SUPERNATURALS (PARANORMAL
PRISON): BOOK 2

LACEY CARTER ANDERSEN

DEDICATION

To my husband—thanks for always inspiring me to keep going.

~ Lacey Carter Andersen

WANT MORE FROM LACEY CARTER ANDERSEN?

Sign up for exclusive first looks at my hot new releases, exclusives, and contests from Lacey Carter Andersen!

Want to be part of the writing process? Maybe even get a taste of my sense of humor? Teasers for my new releases? And more? Join Lacey's Realm on Facebook!

1

ELIZABETH

I thought the soft laughter I heard was only in my mind, but when all my guys stiffen, I realized that it wasn't. Something's in the shadows. And given what we've been through, it probably isn't good.

"I'll check it out," Gabriel whispers, taking a step toward the darkness.

I grab a hold of his shirt, keeping him close, beneath the false safety of the lone bulb. "No, we made it this far because we stayed together, we're not separating now."

Part of me couldn't believe everything we'd been through. I'd been taken to Nightmare Penitentiary just because my strange powers had led me to the park filled with dead supernaturals. I'd been thrown into the prison only to run into my ex-boyfriend Gabriel and his buddies. And together we'd not only created a powerful bond, but we'd managed to escape. Not just the prison, but the horrifying death that all the other prisoners in our area of the prison had suffered.

And then? *Then* we'd been caught by the warden and his guards only to wake up here.

In *another* prison.

Fate was a cruel bitch.

"Who's there?" I call, trying to keep my voice firm.

Ax and Blade move to stand at our sides.

No one answers.

My gaze moves between my men, trying to unbiasedly evaluate how much of a threat someone might regard them as. Gabriel is the largest of them by far, and the dark fae naturally radiates the kind of energy that screams, "I can kill you with a glance," which he actually can. Blade is nearly as tall, but he's more muscular. His blond hair contradicts with Gabriel's dark brown hair, and he has the rough exterior of someone who never loses a fight. Ax... well, Ax looks more like a supermodel, with his jet black hair, and his tightly muscled body. And yet, right now, every muscle in his body is tensed. And then there's me... well, I doubted an average-sized woman was frightening. But I thought our group would be enough to discourage anything that might be waiting for us in those shadows.

So bring it, bitch, I think, glaring into the darkness, and then looking back at my crew.

Blade turns to face me, and I gasp, grabbing his arm.

We all look down at once only to notice the strange curling tattoo that covers his arm. And before I can ask him where it came from, I see that Ax and Gabriel have matching tattoos on their own arms. My stomach turns as I look down and see the same tattoo on myself. Not only have we all been marked against our will, but I'm no longer wearing my prison uniform. Someone has dressed me in a clean, form-fitting black tank top, that's cut-off to expose my belly, long tight black pants, and black army boots. My men wear longer tight black tank tops and black pants with boots.

"They *changed* us and *tattooed* us?" I can't keep the horror from my voice.

"When I get my hands on those fucking bastards—" Gabriel sounds like he wants to kill someone, and I know the dark fae well enough to know he'd follow through with his threat, if he could.

"At least we're clean," Ax cuts-in, but I can tell the shapeshifter is trying to force the humor into his voice.

"Wherever we are. No matter the twisted reason we're here, we need to get out," Blade says, and the half-vampire, half-shifter shivers. I wonder if it's the chill in this place or if one of his conflicting sides is stretching to life.

"It was a test." A deep voice comes from one of the dark hallways connecting to the circular room.

My men react in an instant, leaping to stand in front of me. Every one of them screams *danger* as they stand, fists clenched, every muscle in their bodies tense, facing an unknown enemy.

I peer around them and into the shadows. "Who's there?"

A man emerges, followed by three others. All of them are large, dirty, and dangerous-looking. Each man has long, dark hair that hangs down over their faces and eyes that are black and soulless.

The largest flashes a smile with a mouth full of pointed teeth. "We? We're, apparently, your competition." His voice is a growl, a threat, and I can feel in my heart that none of them are human, but I don't know what the hell they are.

"What?" I ask, shaking my head, confused and taken off-guard.

He flashes a smile. "Apparently the warden setup tests in several areas of the prison. Anyone who survived was sent down here." His smile widens. "You're the fifth group."

"Fifth?"

"We were the second," another voice says, and my head jerks to the sound.

Five more men emerge from the shadows of another one of the tunnels. They're taller and thinner, and the red rings around their eyes mark them instantly as vampires. But it's their identical striking red hair that surprises me... these men had to be related.

"Those demons were the third group," the vampire continues smoothly, jerking his head toward the massive men who had first spoken to us.

"And we were the fourth," a woman's oddly smooth voice comes from another tunnel.

Three men and a woman emerge from the shadows. I have no idea what the hell they are, but they all carry weapons. Each one of them seems to stand at odds with the others, the woman has blue hair and blue eyes, the man directly at her side has deep auburn hair and strangely auburn eyes. Two men stand off a bit behind them, one with light brown hair and light brown eyes, and the final with pale blonde hair and pale golden eyes. There's something... strange about them. Something I can't quite identify.

My heartbeat quickens. It wasn't the time to study them. It was the time to ask questions. "But why? Why were we all sent down here?"

The largest of the demons, his eyes so dark they're almost black, locks onto me with his unsettling gaze. "Apparently, they have another test for us."

"Which is?"

"My guess?" he flashes a smile of those sharp teeth of his. "A fight to the death."

My stomach flips. "But no one has told us why we're here?"

"No," he continues, "but there are four paths that lead to this room. Paths that seem to go nowhere, except to random rooms of weapons and sleeping areas. If the first test was meant to discover those strongest among the prisoners, it only makes sense that that's what we're doing here too."

I shake my head. "Or maybe this is just another fucked up part of the prison, and there's no plan, just another place we can't escape from."

The demon smiles. "I'm voting for the killing of each other."

"That does seem to be logical," the vampire adds, shooting the demon a disturbed look.

Gabriel seems to swell in front of me, and I wonder if the dark fae will use his unique powers on these men. I hoped not. Not yet. "And until we're told what to do?"

"We return to our tunnels." The demon points to the tunnel we came from. "That is your tunnel. If you go in any other one, expect to die."

"Same goes for you coming anywhere near ours," Gabriel threatens right back.

I get the strange feeling they only emerged from their tunnels to evaluate us. Because with Gabriel's final words, they begin to turn and head back toward the darkness of their designated areas.

But then the woman's voice comes back to me, "but watch out for the ghost. We think he's from the first group that came down here. He's not someone you want to cross."

Ghost? Ghosts I can handle.

When all the strangers are gone from sight, I look back at my men. "What do we do now?"

Blade speaks, his voice tense. "We get ready. Because as much as I don't like that demon scum, I agree with him.

This whole thing speaks of another test. And it's not one we want to fail."

2

STORM

From the shadows, I watch the new group square off with the other four. Over the last few days more prisoners have arrived, and I've taken as little interest in them as I have in the ones before. I find it humorous that they think there have only been five groups. I wonder what they would say if they knew there had been dozens?

Dozens of strong warriors.

Dozens of horrible deaths.

In the past, I sometimes warned them. I saw their futures like a movie reel. I watched them die and woke in a sweat. Like a crazed man, I tried to save them, even though I knew the truth. It didn't matter what I did, they would die.

There was only one death that stood out for me from the others. Because her death changed. Every time the visions of her came, they were different. Never in the hundreds of years that I've lived had a Death Vision changed. I had begun to believe the vision wasn't real. That she was a hallucination brought about by all the horror I had seen in my long life.

And then *she* had appeared.

This strange woman has flowing red hair and brilliant blue eyes that call to me. Unlike other visions, I swore the woman who appeared in this prison was different than the person in my mind. In the visions, I felt curious about her. With her standing in front of me, I felt attraction, fascination, and an odd respect. And the wolf within me? He seemed to stand at attention.

And then there was the way the three massive males responded to her, which seemed illogical. When had big males ever been cowered by a tiny female before?

They stand illuminated beneath the one light in this dark place. I watch them like a play.

"I guess we go to our tunnel and try to find the weapons?" she asks, her voice like music after so long spent surrounded by other males.

The big man that stands in front of her has dark brown hair and grey eyes. I'm startled when I see those eyes of his. *Is he truly a dark fae?* Their kind were rare and few people respected them. But in my life, I had met a few that made me realize two things: not all of them were evil, but *all* of them were dangerous.

It's strange the way my heart beats faster as he leans over her, closer to her. "We should find out everything we can. The other groups have been here longer, that's an advantage."

"And we should stay together," another says.

This man makes the hairs on my spine stand on end. Visually, there's nothing off about him. He has dirty-brown colored hair, slicked back from his face and a little long. The style draws attention to the sharp lines of his face, which are softened only by a slight beard. He looks ragged and dangerous, but there's nothing that should make me react in such a way.

So, I inhale slowly and feel my eyes widen. *He's a shifter? But something else... something wrong.*

My lips curl. A mixed breed then. My gut reaction is to want him as far as possible from the fascinating woman, and yet, I'm never quick to act. My wolf might urge me to tear his throat open, but I grit my teeth and remain where I stand, ignoring my angry wolf prowling inside of me.

As she smiles tentatively up at him and says, "of course. We're a team," his eyes soften, and I realize that perhaps he's not the crazed beast that are often the offspring of mixed breeds. Which is... unusual. Not unheard of, but unusual.

My gaze slides to the remaining man. *Are they all exceptions to the rules I've come to believe then? And how did such a strange mix of supernaturals come together?*

"We're going to be okay," the final man says, grinning. "Worst case scenario, I just grow and bring the roof down on this place."

The black-haired man with his cool-blue eyes surprises me. Not only does it sound like he's a shapeshifter, but he smiles down here? In *this* place? That in itself made him unusual. In the darkness, it's rare for any flower to bloom.

This group. They were different from the others. *But how? And what brought them here?*

It'd been a long time since I felt it useful to speak to any of the competitors in this dark place. But no matter how much I try to convince myself that speaking to them will be no different than it had been with the other groups, I knew I had to.

I also knew for some strange reason, I *wanted* them to survive.

I rise from where I crouch, my body shifting from the grey of the shadows to its true brilliant snow-white shade. Within me, my beast stirs, and I wonder what he'll say when he smells her. I wonder if he'll feel the same curiosity as I do.

Moving out from the shadows, it's the dark fae that sees me first. He moves to block my view of the woman, and his eyes hold a threat. Other creatures might not realize the threat they face in that moment, but I do. Within myself, I feel him reaching inside of me, ready to end my life with a thought should I prove to be a danger.

"Hello," I say, and my voice is craggy with misuse.

"Who the fuck are you?" he growls, his eyes narrowing, and his powers fill the room like a bubble.

"I'm called many things," I say. The female peers around him, and those blue eyes of hers look at me with curiosity rather than fear. Which is another surprise.

"Care to elaborate?" The shapeshifter asks, humor in his voice.

"My mother named me Storm," even though no matter how hard I tried I couldn't remember her face. "The competitors simply call me the Ghost."

The woman gives a hesitant smile. "I'm Elizabeth, and this is Gabriel," she says pointing to the dark fae, "and this is Blade," she introduces the mixed shifter, "and this is Ax," she tells me finally, indicating the shapeshifter.

I give a slight bow, even though I know that's no longer the custom. "My lady."

Her cheeks heat. "How long have you been down here, Storm?"

I'm surprised how distracted I am by the way she says my name. "Too long."

"Then... do you know why we're down here?"

"Yes." I wish I could lie to her, but that's not my way. "You're all here to die."

The shifter steps closer to me and flashes... fangs? *Holy hell, a half-shifter half-vampire?* I had never met one of those. "Is that a threat?"

I shake my head. "It's a fact. Five groups are brought down at a time. They compete in different tests. And they all die. Over and over again."

The small woman, this Elizabeth, moves around her men. "Well, we survived Nightmare Penitentiary, we even escaped, so we don't plan to die here either."

"This is Nightmare Penitentiary."

Her jaw drops. "What? But we..."

"It's far beneath the surface of the prison. There are, in fact, many levels beneath the prison."

She closes her mouth, and I hate the doubt that comes and goes across her face. "Well, it doesn't matter. We'll survive this too." Her gaze locks with mine too. "You survived here. Maybe you could tell us how?"

I wished I could. But every vision I saw of her future ended in death.

"I can't help you," I say, and it hurts to speak the words.

For some reason, I feel tired. Unreasonably tired.

I slip back into the shadows of the demons' tunnel.

"Wait," she calls.

I pause.

"If you change your mind, you know where to find us."

Slipping into the darkness, I let my skin change to blend in with the shadows. I race until I come to the opening, and I leap. Above the demon's tunnels, I'd found a place to hide that led me through all the competitors' tunnels. Here, I waited until I had to fight again. Usually, it was dull and miserable. But now that I met the strange woman from my Death Visions, it felt wrong.

Am I really just biding my time in a place I can never escape?

Or am I running away?

3

ELIZABETH

I t takes a long time to make our way through the tunnels in the darkness, but eventually, we find the weapon's room. I'm shocked when Ax manages to make a torch out of different items in the room, but unbelievably grateful. This place was creepy and unsettling enough without adding the whole pitch black thing to the mix. We all arm ourselves, with daggers on our waists and swords on our backs. Down here there isn't anything easy like a gun. There are, however, things like axes and bows and arrows… basically, weird weapons.

Which I hate to admit, leads me to think this really is just another test area.

"You know that Ghost probably just kills everyone," Gabriel says, and there's an edge to his voice.

I shake my head. "I didn't get that sense from him."

"Sense?" Gabriel looks annoyed as he runs his fingers through his dark hair. "Listen, Elizabeth, we can't keep sugarcoating things for you. You're going to have to toughen up a hell of a lot faster, and that includes not automatically trusting weird men you meet in prisons."

"If I didn't trust weird men I met in prisons, I wouldn't be here with any of you right now," I say, and I know I sound a little smug.

Ax laughs. "She's got you there."

Gabriel sighs. "What I'm trying to say is that I've seen a lot of darkness in this world, and it's kept me alive. If we're going to make it out of here, you're going to have to trust that we might know more about all of this than you do."

My gaze runs over the three men, and I realize that they all feel the same way. It bugs me that they think they know so much better than I do, but then again, they aren't exactly wrong. Growing up pretending to be human, doing normal things like getting good grades, and going off to college, hasn't exactly prepared me for fighting to the death in a prison.

"Okay," I say, slowly, "I get it. But I'm not just here for the ride. I'm useful."

"Whatever the hell wraith powers you have," Blade says, his gaze holding mine. "They're more than just a *little* useful. They saved all of our lives once. They just might do it again."

He's right. I still might not have the greatest control over my powers, nor did I really know their true limitations, but blowing up stuff was a pretty useful power... plus the whole absorbing souls to use like batteries for my magic. I just wanted to be sure the guys remembered I was useful, which, apparently, they did.

I feel my cheeks heat. "So, we're all on the same page then. I'm a badass."

Ax grins and presses away from the wall of the room. A second later, he kisses me until I can't even feel the stone under my feet. The pressure of his lips, the taste of him, is so unbelievably incredible that I'm lost in his touch, for how long I have no idea. But when he releases me, I sag against him for a second panting.

"And I've got mad skills of my own," he says, his voice low and husky.

When I look up at him, he's grinning like a fool.

I laugh and punch him playfully.

Blade clears his throat; the vampire doesn't look impressed with any of this. "I'm thinking we need to figure out what the hell people eat down here."

As if my stomach just realizes that it's hungry, I hear it growl.

All of them hear it, but they're smart enough not to comment.

"If we could find Storm, we could ask..."

"Maybe we figure it out rather than asking the creepy guy," Ax says, rubbing the back of his neck like he's really hoping his suggestion doesn't start another fight.

I disagree, but I keep my mouth shut, remembering how I'd just a second before agreed to trust them a little more. "So, then, we explore and see what we missed now that we have a torch and weapons?"

They nod, and we head out the door of the weapon's room. The main branch of our tunnel breaks off into small branches. One area, near the weapons sections, has a collection of dusty pillows and blankets. Another area has... something like a small lake in one corner of the room. I take one step toward it and something splashes in the water. Gabriel is yanking me back within a split second.

"Food?" I ask, heart racing.

His face is a mask. "If there's nothing else."

We find another split off from the main tunnel. The entire room is covered in strange vines that tangle around every inch of the walls. Some of the vines are green, but most of them are a strange off-brown color. I touch the wall, leaning closer to inspect it as Ax carries the torch just a little further away, to inspect the back wall.

Are there... leaves tangled in the vines? How the hell did leaves get down here?

I open my mouth to ask the question aloud when two eyes flash open in the wall. A scream tears from my lips, and I stumble back.

"What's wrong?" Gabriel's at my side in an instant.

I point at the wall.

Suddenly, the room seems to shift. Huge creatures rip free from the wall. Beings covered in dirt and vines. A dozen creatures with glowing red eyes.

I'm pulling out my sword in an instant, even though I have no idea how the hell to use it. Behind me, I hear the hiss of metal that I hope means the others are pulling out their swords too.

One of the creatures grunts and cocks its head strangely.

"What are they?" I ask, heart racing.

"Sentient Beings," Blade murmurs behind me, and I feel his back press against mine.

"What does that mean?"

"Trouble," Blade whispers. "Get ready to fight or die."

In an instant, the creatures seem to move as one. I reach for my magic, but it seems to slip through my fingertips as my heartbeat fills my ears. I tell myself to calm down and focus, but then they're on us. Their arms reach out for us, but I clumsily swing my sword, and the metal sinks into one of the tangled being's arms.

I expect it to hiss, shriek, or *something*. I *don't* expect it to simply ignore my weapon and wrap its arms around me. I struggle to pull my sword free, reaching around the creature's huge body, but the blade won't budge. The arms that wrap around me tighten, and suddenly I'm being dragged away. The darkness closes around me as I move out of the light from the torch. I try to scream out for help, but the arms are crushing my torso, making it impossible.

The sounds of fighting grow dimmer, and then I hear something splash and a garbled growl that comes from something in the darkness ahead of me. *Is it taking me to that creepy black water?* My blood runs cold. I fight harder, exhausting the last of my strength, but the creature that holds me is like a wall of stone.

The splashing intensifies, and now I know I hear the deep rumble of something growling ahead of me in the darkness. Wherever this creature is taking me, whatever it has planned for me, it can't be good. And I'm completely helpless, just struggling to pull in breaths, unsure if the darkness around me is just the dark, or if I'm starting to lose consciousness.

And then I'm ripped away from the creature.

I'm thrown against a stone wall, and I'm not even able to cry out against the pain, I just lie still, gasping in air. The sounds of a struggle come from just in front of me, and then a garbled scream splits the air, followed by silence. A whimper slips from my lips, and I wince as I struggle to sit up, even though my chest aches, and my body hurts from where it struck the stone.

When warm, strong arms lift me, I strike out on instinct, but there's only a grunt from the creature that holds me. I'm being carried somewhere, but I don't know where, until I suddenly come out into the blinding brightness of the big room that connects all the tunnels. That lone bulb sears my pupils for a moment before my eyes adjust, and then I'm looking up into the face of Storm.

The man has a wound across his face, blood drips from

the open wound, painting his pale cheek. But he doesn't seem to notice it as he looks down at me. "Are you okay?"

I nod, but I'm completely confused. *How did he know I was in trouble? And why did he help me?* "Why did you—?"

"Elizabeth!" I hear Gabriel roar my name from somewhere far behind me.

The guys!

My head jerks to the sound, and I struggle out of Storm's arms. I start forward, but Storm catches my arm. "What are you doing?"

I look back at him. "I have to help them."

"You can't help them."

I snatch my arm away. "Like hell."

Racing back the way I came, I try not to be unnerved by how the shadows close around me. I just run toward the source of light somewhere in front of me. It only takes me seconds to explode back into the room with the sentient beings and my men.

A scream gets caught in my throat. They're surrounded, wounded, and in trouble!

I reach out with my powers... and feel nothing. *Oh fucking hell, the creatures aren't living.* My powers won't work on them. That's probably also why Gabriel couldn't just kill them with a thought.

Grabbing one of the daggers, I start forward, not knowing how the hell I can stop this. Suddenly, a massive pure white wolf, the size of a bear, leaps out in front of me. He tears into one of the creatures, and breaks its strange head off with his massive jaw. The creature crumbles to the floor, but he's not done.

And within seconds, the tide changes.

My men manage to hack down some of the creatures while the wolf tears them apart. Any time one of the beings tries to rise from the ground, I'm there with my dagger, keeping them down. Hacking at their heads until the creatures are just pieces and the bodies stop moving.

And then just as suddenly as the creatures had seemed to awaken, they stilled, all the life gone from them. The ground is littered with debris, and splatters of our blood. And the one lone torch that's been left on the ground makes the shadows around us dance.

We're all breathing hard, tense, looking around us as if waiting for the next attack.

But the wolf? It starts to shift. And within seconds, Storm is crouched in the wolf's place. He rises, naked and as pale as the snowy wolf's fur. My gaze runs from his huge shoulders, down his muscled chest, and then lingers on his massive cock.

I stand slowly, not knowing what to say or do.

Gabriel is suddenly at my side. There's a deep wound on his arm, as if torn into his flesh by sharp wood, but he doesn't seem to notice. He cups my face, and there's fear in his eyes. "Are you okay? Are you hurt?"

I shake my head.

"I saw one of them take you, but I couldn't—"

"It's okay, Storm got me."

Gabriel tenses, and I realize I said the wrong thing. His gaze snaps to the shifter. "Thank you for your help, but we've got it from here."

Storm looks from him to me.

Blade wipes blood away from a cut above his eye, smearing it across his forehead. "Yeah, we got this."

Storm hesitates a moment longer, then turns around and heads back out of the cavern.

"Thank you," I mumble out.

He glances back at me. "No, thank you. Thank you for not dying."

And on those cryptic words, he disappears.

Ax races to my side. "Are you sure you're okay?"

I nod and rub the back of my neck. I'm a little sore, but I was definitely lucky. "You guys do realize you're the ones bleeding and injured, right?"

Ax shrugs. "We're also not human. We'll heal faster than you will."

He's got a point there, although I'm *technically* not human, I just wasn't blessed with the ability to heal quickly. I glance at the sentient beings on the ground. "How worried do we have to be about these things coming after us again?"

Everyone looks at Gabriel, and the muscles in his jaw move. "If we sleep, it should be in shifts."

Ax and Blade nod, and then Ax grabs the torch from where it's fallen on the ground. Then, to my surprise, he starts collecting broken branches.

My jaw drops.

He spots me and says, "what? We'll need more torches."

He's right, and I hate that he's right. Just like when I was taken by those Enforcers and thrown into Nightmare Penitentiary, I was going to have to change my perspective to survive. I was going to need to be tougher and stronger than ever before.

So if we had to burn wood that was previously part of moving creatures, I was going to have to deal with just how creepy that was.

4

BLADE

We do our best to clean up the pillows and blankets. Ax does more than just make more torches, he starts a small fire in the pillow room, our new sleeping quarters, and the bright lights, help to make our new prisons feel less filled with secrets. We also found a dead creature set outside our room. A fish with row after row of shark-like teeth. I knew it only as a Flesh Eater, but I was actually grateful to find it and not an Adaro. The second we'd stepped near the black water, I'd felt certain an Adaro slinked beneath the surface.

A shiver ran down my spine. Flesh eaters I could handle, but not the Adaros.

Ax had picked the fish up without a word, cleaned it, and started cooking it over the flames. None of us said what we already knew. That the Ghost had given it to us.

My hands curl into fists at just the thought. I would learn to hunt those waters for food so that I could give Elizabeth fish. She didn't have any need for the Ghost to take care of her. She was my mate, whether our connection complicated my life or not. The shifter side of myself had chosen her, and there could be no other.

Especially not that... shifter. A full-blood who was capable of taking on his other form.

It angered me, even though subconsciously I knew that part of my anger was jealousy. I could neither control my vampire side, nor shift into my other side. So, of course, this Ghost could turn into a massive, pure-white wolf, the size and shape of which I'd never seen before. He was... special. But whatever the hell he was, I didn't like the way he looked at Elizabeth. And even though Ax and Gabriel hid it better than I did, I knew they felt the same way.

Elizabeth stretches beside the fire, and for a minute I'm transfixed by her. She's changing. Yes, she's still a beautiful red-head, but it's more than that. The first time I saw her I sensed innocent, naivety, and a newness to our world that worried me. Now, with her hair drawn back, the tight, revealing black clothes, and the full-sleeve of dark, swirling black tattoos, she looked... tougher. But there was more to it than that.

And then it hit me. That power that Ax could sense when he first met her, I think I could sense some of it too. And I'm not nearly as sensitive to such things, so if I could, her powers must be growing.

Her blue eyes suddenly connect with mine, and then she's standing and moving toward the pile of pillows tucked into one corner. I feel my eyes darken and my dick harden as I watch the sway of her hips, the seductiveness of her body that she seemed completely unaware of.

When she kneels down near me, I don't think, I just draw her onto my lap.

A gasp slips from her lips, and then I'm kissing the sound away. Our lips press together, and hers spread. My tongue darts into her warm mouth. And even though a second ago I'd been overwhelmed by worry, now all I want to do is touch her... taste her.

As our tongues tangle together, I unbutton her tight black pants and slip a hand inside. She shifts, as if to pull away from me, but I dig my hands into the back of her hair and hold her against me. When my hand pushes aside her underwear, and I start to stroke her entrance, she breaks our kiss, her mouth still barely against mine.

"Blade, we can't," she whispers, but the words come out husky.

I push gently inside of her, and she shivers as I stroke my finger over her wet folds. Her eyelids flutter closed, and she says, "oh," followed by a moan of pleasure. I return to kissing her as I push my finger deeper inside her and then begin to fuck her with my hand softly. She moves against me, helping to take me deeper and harder.

At last, I groan, "fuck."

I loved touching her, but I needed my dick inside of her. The desire struck me so powerfully, that I was suddenly having a hard time pulling in air. An image of me and Elizabeth in our cell leaps into my mind. I remember the way her body wrapped me so tightly and how her blood was fucking intoxicating. She tasted of sweetness and sunlight. And our bodies moved together as if it's what we were always meant to do.

My cock aches, and I know I need her. *Now*.

And then my gaze meets Gabriel's. To my surprise, he reaches for the hem of his shirt and draws it off, then comes toward us. His movements are almost as graceful as any shifter, and there's a strength to his form that I admire. Kneeling down near us on the pillows, Elizabeth looks back at him, a question in her eyes.

He's looking at her when he speaks to me. "Keep touching her."

I obey, and he wraps his hand in her hair, pulls her closer to him, and kisses her, long and deep.

My body shudders as I watch him lift her shirt, and reveal her braless breasts under her tank top. His hands close around her breasts, and I continue to stroke her pussy as her body grows even wetter with excitement.

Watching my best friend kiss her and stroke her breasts should've been strange, but instead I find my arousal growing. My cock feels uncomfortable in my pants, practically begging me to be released. And my eyes are locked on the tantalizing sight of them.

Is this what it is to share a woman? If it was, I could handle this. Maybe not if I'd been a full shifter, but for the first time in my life, I'm glad I'm not.

Unable to help myself, I lean forward and start to suck on her perfect breasts, with Gabriel's hands still grasping them tightly. My cock strains even harder within my pants, and I shift, uncomfortable, as my desperation grows. Elizabeth's hands find my pants as if she can read my mind, and she undoes the button and zipper before drawing my cock free.

I feel a shiver travel down my spine that wracks my entire body.

Before I know what I'm doing, Gabriel and I are both working to strip Elizabeth. My gaze catches Ax's. His hand is already wrapped around his naked dick, as he strokes himself watching us. When he undresses, I'm shocked to realize just how eager he is.

Have they shared a woman before? Because I hadn't imagined it'd be this easy.

When we're all naked, Elizabeth is set down in my lap,

facing away from me. I reach around her and return to stroking that sweet pussy of hers. But Gabriel surprises me by using two fingers to press into her channel just below my fingers. She gasps and reaches behind her, grabbing my hair hard as she pants.

Ax is standing beside us in an instant, steering her face toward him, and suddenly she's hungrily sucking his cock. My own dick swells painfully, and I ache deep inside to bury myself inside her. My gaze sweeps back to Gabriel, he's looking between Elizabeth and me, and I realize that he's working her ass with his other hand too. The thought of it sends my head spinning, and my free hand grips her hip harshly for a minute, while I try not to spill my seed too quickly.

Then, I let one hand travel to her breasts and tease the hard peaks as I try to focus on her pleasure and not my own. But when she starts to thrust against our hands, dragging her ass back and forth on my length, a string of curses explodes from my lips, and I have to consciously work to calm myself down.

But then, someone grabs my dick.

My gaze slams down, and I'm shocked to see Gabriel pushing the tip into Elizabeth's ass. I've never had a man touch me like this. I've never had a desire for anything of the sort. But the fact that he sinks me inch by inch deeper into my mate makes me forget that it's his hand on me, I'm just clinging to my woman until she reaches my hilt.

I'm breathing hard when Gabriel pushes her back on me, forcing Ax to shift or lose the warm mouth around his dick. When Gabriel climbs on top of her, he doesn't hesitate to plunge deep into her pussy, which tears a scream of pleasure from Elizabeth's lips. She begins to move between the two of us, and all three of us thrust in and out of her, drawing out her pleasure and our own.

Stars dance in front of my vision. I sink my teeth into her neck, making us both shudder, and I drink in the sweetness of her blood while I fuck her ass harder.

Had I thought our first time together was amazing? *This... this is everything and more.*

And when I watch Ax come into her waiting mouth, I can't hold back any longer, I explode into her ass. Gabriel continues to thrust into her harder and harder, and then they both crash over the edge together, crying out in unison.

When we're all done, we collapse back onto the pillows, with Gabriel and I still buried inside of her. My thoughts spin, and I draw my teeth from her neck. Closing my eyes, I take a mental picture of the three of us together. Whatever the warden had planned for us down here, it wasn't good.

So I'd take this moment while I can.

5

ELIZABETH

As I lie, sweaty and satisfied between my men, my gaze returns to the shadowy corner in the room where Storm has been watching us. Somehow, like a chameleon, he's blended in with the darkness. If I hadn't caught the flash of his eyes, if I hadn't been watching when he undid his pants and pulled his huge cock free, I wouldn't have known he was there.

But instead, as Blade fucked my ass, Gabriel claimed my pussy, and Ax owned my mouth, I'd let me gaze stray to Storm working his cock. When he'd bit down and cum had exploded from his tip, I'd helped send my own orgasm over the edge. And now, as I shook from the overload of desire, I found myself confused.

Storm had probably been down here for a long time. It'd probably been even longer since he fucked someone. So, it made sense why he'd jerked off in a corner while watching us. What didn't make sense as why I hadn't told the guys, or even tried to stop him. I'd...enjoyed it.

I almost groan. I was already trying to work things out

with these three. I didn't need to add a new, mysterious, man to the mix.

As Storm fixes his pants and slips back out of our room, I feel a wave of disappointment, which is even more confusing. *Were we just a good show? Or was Storm actually attracted to me? And why did it matter?*

Ax sighs. "You guys ready to eat?"

Eating sounded amazing and would definitely help distract me from spinning out about Storm. "Hell, yeah."

The guys seem reluctant as they pull out of me, and we all dress slowly. Ax chars the fish a little more, something about sanitizing it after dropping it on the floor, and then we all eat. I expected the freaky fish to taste like hell. Instead, I'm surprised by how much it reminds me of chicken.

When we're all done, I feel surprisingly full for how little food we'd eaten. Gabriel and Blade take a torch and come back a while later with a couple bowls full of the black water. We wash up with one of the bowls and use the other to drink. I'm relieved to see most of their wounds from the sentient beings have already healed, leaving behind pale pink scars on the guys that I knew would soon fade into nothing.

And then, finally, we lie down together in the pillows. They seem to surround me, holding me as if I'm the most important thing in the world. And for a time, I almost forget that it's weird that I have three men. I almost forget that we're prisoners of some psycho and that I have no idea what tomorrow will bring. I just sleep.

And I've never been more content in my life.

But like all good things, it had to end.

6

GABRIEL

None of us told Elizabeth, but we'd already agreed on our shifts. Our races didn't seem to need quite as much sleep as Elizabeth, so we divided our sleeping time the best we could in a place where it could've been day or night. I took the last shift, mostly because Ax and Blade had agreed I had the worst wounds and needed the most time to heal. For once I hadn't argued. Whatever tomorrow would bring, I needed to be able to protect Elizabeth.

And I couldn't do that properly while wounded.

So when it was my turn, I set more wood on the fire and remained by the flames. My gaze moved from the shadows that surrounded us to my best friends and my woman. It was strange. Just a short time ago I couldn't imagine sharing her. But now? Now, I couldn't imagine a life *without* all of us in a relationship together. I only hoped our connection strengthened us, not weakened us.

Ax seemed to toss and turn for a while, unable to sleep after his shift. I was surprised and a little fascinated when he turned Elizabeth around, took off their pants, and slid into her. Within seconds, she was moaning, her eyes fluttering open a few times as Ax fucked her with abandon. When a short time later, she cried out, I watched him come inside of her.

Then, silently, Ax dressed them both. He pulled her against him, and Blade lay on her other side, out cold. The strangest thing of all was that he never opened his eyes. It was as if something inside of him couldn't relax until he'd fucked our woman.

Are we all so completely smitten with her?

When all of them were breathing silently, I tugged out my own cock and moved to a corner. Pressing a hand to the wall, and looking back at them, it took only seconds to lose control. My desire painted the wall, and I took several long shuddering breaths, trying to figure out why the hell I was so damned turned on.

I washed up the best I could after, and sat down before the fire again, satisfied and oddly happy. As sad as it was, today was the freest I'd been in all my life. I'd told Elizabeth more about me, more about my life with my dark fae mother, and about how she had abandoned me, but I didn't tell her everything. Not even close.

And I'd meant it when I'd said we understood danger, pain, and this world better than her. I only prayed she'd listen to us when the time came.

A few hours later, a strange staticky crackling destroyed the silence. All of us were standing in an instant. I could see the panic in their gazes as we all resheathed our swords and looked into the darkness for any sign of where the noise was coming from. When nothing appeared, we crept out of our room, ready for battle, and followed the sound until we came to the main room with its lone bulb.

I wasn't surprised to see all the other groups cautiously

gathered in the room too. Our gazes moved up, and I spotted the source of the sound. Before it'd seemed like just part of the ceiling, but now I realized it was some kind of speaker.

What the hell?

Suddenly, a familiar voice oozes out of the speaker. "Welcome, prisoners."

I stiffen. It's garbled and crackly, but I'd know it anywhere.

"The warden," Elizabeth whispers near us.

I don't take my eyes off the speaker. "Congrats... passing.... First test. Now... fun begins.... Pass the test... or die. Good luck."

The garbled, broken string of sentences stops.

"What the hell did that mean?" Blade asks, and his gaze darts around the room.

The ground begins to shake, and a space between two of the tunnels opens into another tunnel, like a stone wall being lifted to reveal the secrets behind.

"We shouldn't go there," the woman with the blue hair says.

Her team nods around her.

"We'll find out what it is," the largest of the demons snarls, "and the rest of you will be punished for your disobedience."

Suddenly, Ghost emerges into the room, as if separating from the shadows themselves. "If you don't go, they'll close the door. The tunnels will be filled with a poisonous gas, and everyone remaining will die."

"Fuck," Elizabeth mumbles.

"So we go?" Ax asks, his gaze locking with mine.

I don't trust the Ghost, but it seems like just the kind of twisted up shit the warden would do, so I nod.

The demons start down the tunnel ahead of us, and we

follow after. The vampires are at our backs, and being surrounded by them makes the hairs on my arms stand on end. My hand clenches and unclenches as I struggle not to reach for my blade. But then I catch a glimpse of the Ghost behind them and some of my tension eases. If he's coming to, this probably is the thing to do. And as much as I didn't like him, it might help to have him at our backs.

I hear someone cry out, and we look back as the group with the woman rush into the tunnel as the door starts to close. For a second, I think one of the men isn't going to make it, but a man with pale blonde hair stretches out his hands and a rush of air keeps the door from closing long enough for a red-haired man to roll under.

And then it closes.

And we're breathing hard. *Elementalists?* Hell, elementalists were rare. And dangerous. It was true they weren't as physically strong as most species, nor did they heal as quickly, but their powers were a force to reckon with.

"Let's keep going," Blade murmurs.

I nod, but promise myself to keep my eye on them. We continue down the torch-lined hall until we exit out of a strange room. The circumference of the room is about the same as the other main room. It's enough room to contain all of us, with extra left over, but not much. But what's strange about it is how tall the room is. It towers above us, two, three, four stories tall. And at the very top, bright torches burn.

"What the fuck is this?"

Every group moves into the room and starts to drift around, frowning as they glance around, probably as confused as I am.

Then, Ghost is at Elizabeth's side. He whispers into her ear, and I'm there in an instant shoving him back and pinning him against the wall by the throat. "Don't. Ever. Touch. Her." I growl in warning.

I sense in the big man the strength to shove me away, but his gaze simply locks with mine, a challenge in his pale eyes. Like one wolf challenging another.

Elizabeth is there in an instant. She grabs onto my arm, and I can't help but turn to her.

Her face is pale, and my hand squeezes tighter around the man's throat. "What's wrong?"

She leans closer and whispers in my ear, her hot breath tickling my skin. "He says to start climbing. Now."

I frown. *Climbing?* I glance again at the walls and see that the ends of wood boards are sticking out in various places in the stone, leading all the way up to the top.

I'm still processing his words when the room begins to shake and a stone wall closes us off from the tunnel we'd come through, trapping us in the room. Above us, a small platform emerges from the wall nearly at the top. Elizabeth has gone to whisper in Ax's and Blade's ears. They're all looking at me now.

I glance back at the wolf. "If you're lying to us..."

"I'm not."

I release him and gesture to the others. We start climbing, even though I'm still not sure what the hell we're doing or why. The small ends of woods we have to use are difficult to stay on, and the wood is stretched far enough apart that I feel sweat roll down my back after no time at all. *Will Elizabeth even be able to do this?*

She's beside me, and I find myself hauling her higher every time she can't reach another piece of wood. Blade is on her other side, and Ax beside him. And to my surprise, Ghost climbs at my side. He doesn't look the least bit nervous, or like this is dangerous. Instead, he seems to be climbing and waiting for us.

Which is weird.

I hear a demon laugh beneath us. "Look at them, like fucking monkeys."

"Why are you climbing?" The female Elementalists asks, and there's concern in her voice.

But it's a vampire that answers, his tone mocking. "A better question is how they survived Nightmare Penitentiary long enough to be sent here."

And then a strange clicking sound radiates through the room below us. For the first time, I chance a glance down. Small holes have opened near the bottom of the room. *What the hell?* And then, water begins to pour from them, so rapidly that it seems to rush out like a storm.

The elementalists leap onto the wall and start climbing on Ghost's side. The vampires and shifters go to the holes that are pouring water, frowning.

Ghost speaks from beside me. "Faster. Get her higher!"

My stomach turns, and I start moving again. Elizabeth struggles, but either Blade or I are there every time she might slip, pinning her back to the wall with our hands. She's breathing hard, we all are, and we're not even close to the top.

I hear the vampires grumbling beneath us, and I don't need to look down to know that they've started climbing on the wall across from us.

The female elementalist cries out, and I chance a glance to see that she's fallen. She starts to climb again, but the wood piece she was standing on disappears back into the wall. Her eyes widen in fear, and she gestures to the water. A second later, it lifts her up, and she leaps, catching the wall.

I turn away from them and keep going. If these wooden planks disappear...

"Faster!" I order the others.

And we all pick up our paces.

Beside me, I can feel Ghost's gaze moving from me to Elizabeth.

Beneath us, I hear the demons finally starting to scramble. A small hiss comes, and I glance down again to see more wooden planks near the bottom disappear. The demons fall, unable to grab onto the planks. They start to jump. The water reaches their knees, and they struggle to use the stone to pull themselves up, but can't. The lowest wooden planks are just a little too high to reach.

I hear the female Elementalist, her voice just loud enough for me to hear. "Don't fall. I can use the water to lift us up, but it might help the demons too..."

My blood runs cold, and I chance a look around the room. There's no way in hell all of us can climb on the walls and stay above the planks that are disappearing. If the demons were lifted this high, they'd have to pull some of us down to secure their spots.

"Faster," is all I can say.

But I feel the tension in our group. We all heard the Elementalist. We all know right now some of us are going to live and some of us are going to die.

We'll be the group that lives. We *had* to be.

Beneath us, the demons bellow in rage, but I don't chance another glance down. We don't have time.

7

ELIZABETH

My legs and arms are shaking with exhaustion, and I'm suddenly regretting blowing off PE so much as a kid. Hell, I'm regretting eating donuts while on my exercise bike back at my apartment. If someone had told me that I might need to climb a steep wall to survive, I would've done more than just judo half-heartedly to stay fit. I'd actually have focused on strength training.

But now it didn't matter. I just had to keep going.

One of my hands slips, and my life flashes before my eyes for a split second before Gabriel's hand grabs the back of my shirt, keeping me from falling long enough for me to get my grip again. I do, and I grit my teeth, trying to pull my heart out of my stomach. I might be the weak link here in some ways, but I'd be damned if I didn't try my hardest.

The demons are going crazy beneath us. I make the mistake of looking down and a squeak of fear explodes before I can stop it. We're halfway to the top. Easily two stories high. Beneath us, the water has reached the throats of the demons. They're racing around, the best that they can in water, and desperately trying to reach any pieces of wood. But the wood planks disappear about ten steps below us, way too high for the demons. The water might not kill them, but I'm sure something in this sick game will.

"Don't look at them, keep going." I'm surprised when I look over and see Storm watching me.

But he's right, so I keep pushing myself higher. I try to ignore the way the demons' voices go from angry to fearful. Yet when I hear a vampire scream, I can't help but turn the best I can and look toward the sound. I see one the vampires plummet into the water far below. Instantly the demons attack, and I'm shocked when the water turns red.

One of the demons locks eyes with me and licks the blood clean from his claw, smiling.

I'm shaking even harder as I keep climbing.

Another vampire screams and falls. *They started too late.* I realize that now. The wooden planks they're standing on are disappearing into the wall. If they can't get higher faster, they're all going to fall into the water with the blood-thirsty demons.

Only this time when the vampire falls, he's ready for a fight. I can hear the snarling and commotion below me, but I keep going higher, knowing I can't afford to be distracted.

"The vampires will fall first," Storm says, "then the Elementalists, if they can't go faster."

He doesn't sound the least bit out of breath. Which is pretty damned annoying when I'm wheezing like I'd just finished chasing a car with a sign that says, "Free Chocolate Cake."

Storm keeps talking, as if he doesn't realize that him being in shape is annoying the crap out of me. "Anyone who doesn't reach the plank above us in time will be sealed up in this room, full of water. They'll drown."

Wait... what?

"Fuck," Ax pants near me.

I swear our group moves even faster.

And then, I hear a terrible sound of cruel amusement under me. I glance down and see that one of the demons has stood on the shoulders of one of his brothers. He gets his balance... and jumps. He manages to grab onto one of the wooden planks far under me. As I watch, he uses his impressive upper-body strength to pull himself all the way up and reach for the next plank.

A terrible thought enters my mind. I want that plank he clings to to disappear. I want... and then he reaches the next plank and grins. Slowly, he makes his way up right under me, and I realize that if he overtakes me he'll probably toss me right into the water. My stomach churns as I try to keep my hands, slick with sweat, on my plank and use my feet to push me higher.

Time ticks away. I sense him beneath me, but I'm getting closer and closer to freedom. To the platform above. It's no more than a story above me. If I can just keep going. If I can just...

Something wraps around my ankle.

I look down and the grinning demon tightens his hold on me.

"No!" almost slips from my lips, but before it can, he yanks me down.

Maybe if I'd just started climbing, maybe if I'd been in better shape, maybe if I wasn't so damned tired, I could've held on. But instead, he pulls me off, and suddenly I'm falling. I see the moment my men turn and see me, but I'm already gone, already too far to save. I hit the water so hard it steals my breath. Blood clouds around me, and the vampires' lifeless bodies drift. Their white, wispy spirits surround them for one powerful moment before they press into me.

And it's that alone that gives me the energy to swim for the surface. It's that power alone that gives me the strength to shake off the shock of my fall. I almost explode free of the water when a huge hand clamps down on top of my head and starts to push me under again.

I struggle. I scream beneath the water, but the leering faces of the demons is all I can see.

And I know. I know. I'm going to die.

8

AX

Watching Elizabeth fall is one of the worst moments in my life. The fear in her face, the utter horror, is like a dagger to my heart. I reach for her, even though I can't save her, and watch her hit the water.

"So this is how she dies. It's too bad," Ghost says near me.

"Shut up!" I snarl.

Gabriel reaches a hand down and points at the demon who pulled our Elizabeth down from the wall. The demon has the nerve to grin up at us. Something cold and expressionless comes over Gabriel's face, and then he makes a smooth motion.

The demon dies. He doesn't even have the time to realize it when the life fades from his face, and he falls down from the wall like an empty sack of flesh... which is all he is now.

Beneath us, Elizabeth hasn't yet surfaced, but I can sense the demons that surround her.

I see Gabriel point his hand down at the water and twist his wrist. A second later a demon leaps from the ever-deepening water screaming. Blood fills his eyes, and then Gabriel motions with his hand again, and the demon dies. Then, he moves his hand again to point at another spot in the water, and I know he's feeling for the mind of the next demon. But while I know he can kill the demons from here, Elizabeth is still lost to us if we can't get her up here.

We need to try to save her. *But how?*

And then, it hits me.

"I'm going to get her," Blade says, before I can. In his face, I see his acceptance that this might kill him, but I know he'll still try. He'd do anything for his mate.

Luckily for him, I'd do anything for her too.

"You can't get back up," I tell him. "But I can."

Blade's gaze holds mine for a second before I see him realize that it can be only me. But I know from the expression on his face that he doesn't fully understand. Yes, I can save her. But I don't know if I'll make it back myself.

"Wish me luck," I say, and then I kick off the wall, aiming to fall far enough from where she dropped to keep from hitting her.

The air sails around me, and then I hit the water with all the force of a brick wall. The air knocks from my lungs for a horrible second before I recover, and then I search the waters. My gut churns when I spot Elizabeth surrounded by demons, but anger quickly replaces my worry. I clench my fists and focus on my abilities. Needing to grow, but not so fast as to bring the walls down on us all.

I expand slowly, reaching out a hand to grasp Elizabeth as I rise. A demon tries to take her from me, but I'm easily four times his size already. I knock him away, and he hits the wall and doesn't move. Another demon in the water suddenly stops moving, his body floating to the surface. I close my hand around Elizabeth as my size increases, and then I'm pulling us both out of the water, my feet solidly on the ground.

Where one minute only the top half of my body is free from the water, I continue to grow and grow until my head nearly reaches the top of the huge room. I reach for the little platform near the top and spot an open doorway in the wall. With cautious movements, I set Elizabeth down on the platform. She tumbles onto it, soaking wet and gasping for air. She looks at me with huge eyes, and I smile, before turning back to the others.

I pluck Gabriel and Ax off the wall, even though I hear their protests, and I set them on the platform too. Then, without thinking, I do the same to Ghost. But rather than looking disturbed, he studies me strangely as he rises to stand on the platform.

Then, taking a deep breath, I focus on saving myself.

Below me, three vampires still climb the wall. On the other side, the Elementalists are staying ahead of the disappearing wooden steps. And in the water below, dead demons and vampires float at the top of the ever-rising water.

Taking a deep breath, I go back to the wall and try to live, even though every way I imagine doing this ends in my death. I try to slowly shrink and still hold onto the pillars. But I'm too big when I'm still able to reach them for them to be able to support my weight. But when I let myself shrink smaller, I can't reach them anymore.

I try shrinking and growing over and over again as the water continues to rise, but no combination ends in me being able to climb out. At last, I go to my normal size and look up. The Elementalists have reached the platform and take off down the hall. The remaining vampires are nearly there. But Elizabeth, Gabriel, Blade, and the Ghost remain on it, staring down at me.

Ghost looks troubled.

The others look horrified.

A strange fluttering fills my chest. For a minute my life seems to flash before my eyes. There was still so much I wanted to do. So much I wanted to say.

I think of my wife. I think of the day I came home to her lover standing over her dead body. I still don't remember killing him, but I remember that my voice was hoarse and my hands were covered in his blood.

And I remember when the police came. I remember when they called it a crime of passion and accused me of killing them both. They'd said I did what all shapeshifters did, I killed. None of them wanted to believe that even though I'd married the woman just to appease my parents and our people, I'd cared for her. I'd known about the affair. And I'd always thought that we'd both eventually admit that it wasn't working and part ways as friends.

I'd never thought that by being too afraid to speak the truth, I might end up on a path I never wanted to be on.

But now, as I look up at my best friends and the woman I love, I can't say that I'm upset about what happened if it led me to them. I can only say that I don't want them to be haunted by my death the way I was haunted by what happened to my wife.

So, I smile. I wave and force myself to pretend my heart isn't racing. I see two of the vampires reach the platform and run down the hall.

"You have to go!" I shout "Before the door closes and we all get stuck here."

Elizabeth shakes her head, and now the water has risen enough that I can see the tears in her eyes as I swim in the ever-rising water. There are only three wooden steps remaining. Once those are gone, I think the door will close too. They don't need to stay here and watch me die.

"Just go," I say.

"Ax," Gabriel calls my name, and the one word is filled with raw emotion.

Suddenly, Ghost stands to his full height, and leaps down from the platform. I'm shocked when his huge body hits the water beside me. I swim back from him the best I can, not knowing what the hell is going on. When he emerges from the water, he's no longer a man, but the massive wolf.

On my back, comes in my mind.

It feels strange. I don't trust him, but I can't explain the fact that he's risking his life, or that he's helping me. So, I swim over and awkwardly climb onto his back.

Hold onto my fur tightly.

I do as the voice in my mind says. The wolf moves to one wall, and I feel all the muscles in his body tighten, and then he uses the wall to leap forward. For a second, I think the water will slow him down too much, but he hits the other side of the room, shaking the very stone, and then begins to leap from one side to the other.

I cling to him, feeling like I'm flying. Feeling like this is some horrible nightmare.

Above us I hear the rumble of the door closing.

"Run!" I scream.

Gabriel throws Elizabeth over his shoulder and then they're all gone. We keep moving, keep leaping from side to side. I have no idea if it's too late. I have no idea if the door has closed, but then we hit the platform, jumping over the final vampire's head. The wolf doesn't slow. He races forward, and we slip just under the door before it closes behind us.

On the other side of the door, we hear someone screaming in outrage or fear, I wasn't sure. We hear pounding on the door, and the hairs on my body stand on end. It's like watching the last breaths of someone you can't save.

Death was never pretty, but something about dying for some unknown person's... amusement, pleasure, or boredom made it even worse. It made me feel torn between sadness and anger.

Ghost turns away from the door, and I'm glad he does, even though the pounding continues. The room we're in with the other survivors is small, cold, and lit by one lone torch. Ghost carries me closer to where Gabriel, Blade, and Elizabeth are. They all stand together in a cold, dripping group. There, we pause, and listen as the pounding grows softer and softer before stopping altogether.

And then, it's silent. Deathly, painfully silent.

I climb off of the wolf, my legs shaking.

Ghost shifts back into a pale, naked man, but doesn't seem to care about his nudity. He stands like a king of the shifters, his hands clenched at his side, his gaze on the door. His face is expressionless, and for a moment, I feel sorry for him. *Is he just alone or is he lonely? And if he'd been here for some time, had he witnessed death many times before this like we had?*

No one speaks. We just all continue staring at the door as time ticks by.

Near me, I hear the vampires giving a prayer for their fallen brothers. "May the Queen of the Darkness watch over their eternal souls. May she have mercy on us all."

"Amen," comes from both the vampires.

More time passes, and we all collapse against the wall in

the darkness. The elementalist woman and her men talk in low voices. The two remaining vampires are painfully silent.

I try to think of something to say to cheer up the others. But after a time, Elizabeth comes to me and wraps me in her arms, her entire body shaking. I'm surprised when I cling to her, when I hold her tight. *I almost died. I almost lost her.*

Next time, we needed to do better.

My gaze connects with the Ghost's, with Storm's. I find it hard to speak, but I do. "Thank you."

He gives a nod. "She didn't die there either. Something is different about you four."

I don't know what he means, so I just hold Elizabeth tighter.

And then the room shakes, and we all leap to our feet. The door to the room begins to open, and I think everyone pictures the same thing I do: the water flooding in here and killing us all.

Instead, it opens into an empty room and the sound of dripping water. We venture hesitantly out onto the platform and look down. The water has emptied from the room. All that remains is water that drips from the walls and the bodies that are crumbled on the floor far below.

"Time to climb down," Storm says.

And this time, our group listens to him and the others follow. We're exhausted, physically, mentally, and emotionally. I can feel it in the air, radiating from my soul, and from the souls of everyone around me. Prisoners weren't exactly the faint of heart, but something about this whole "game" was a kind of evil we weren't prepared for.

We climb down so damned slowly it's a joke, but we finally reach the bottom.

The vampires gather their dead brethren, holding them closely. We all stare at the demons, and I find it damned hard to feel sorry for them. Hell, I kind of want to kick the one that yanked Elizabeth down, but then decide he's dead enough. The opening into the tunnels is there, and we slowly move around the bodies and start back the way we came.

A strange sound comes from behind us. A terrible cracking and spitting of water. A chill rolls down my spine, and I turn slowly back around. Three of the demons are twitching and spitting out water.

No. No way.

The eyes of the one that pulled Elizabeth down flashes open. For one second, they're confused, and then his mouth twists into a smile. The four of them rise like they hadn't just died horribly.

My stomach sinks. There are only a small group of demons who can come back to life like that, and they're children of the Queen of Hell. Powerful demons that are rare and greatly feared. I had no doubt why they were in a prison, the bastards, but I had no clue who thought it was fair to have them competing against the rest of us.

And then they're looking at Gabriel.

"You're a dark fae," the leader says, each word spoken with hatred and fear.

"And you're an asshole."

The demon's black eyes narrow. "The name's Daun."

"Daun?" Gabriel cocks his head. "How many times can you guys die before you stay dead?"

The demon flashes his sharp teeth. "No idea."

Gabriel lifts a hand and slashes it. All four demons crumple again. I catch Gabriel under the arms as he staggers. The guy liked to pretend like he was invincible, but all of us had our limits, and he had reached his.

"That was stupid," I growl at him. "If they're children of

the Queen of Hell, few things can actually kill them for good."

"It was worth it," Gabriel pants.

"Agreed," Storm says softly. "I don't like them."

The female elementalist smiles. "I like you guys," and then her smile falters. "Too bad I'm pretty sure it's you or us."

"Come on, River," the red-haired Elementalist says, and takes her hand.

They walk away and our group follows, along with the vampires who carry their dead. When we nearly reach the main cavern, with its lone blinking bulb, we hear the distinct sounds of the demons coming back to life.

Well, fuck. It looks like we just made some pretty damned dangerous enemies.

And it looks like this is only the first of the things we're going to endure.

I shudder. *Is it really going to get worse?*

9

ELIZABETH

In our tunnel later, I'm lying on blankets with Gabriel and Blade asleep next to me. Ax had requested to take the first shift, and since he'd nearly died, I don't think any of us could refuse him anything. But I can't sleep. I watch him poke at the fire. He's naked and seated on the floor, his clothes drying on the side of the fire, along with mine. I grab the little blanket that's over me and wrap it around myself, then go and sit next to him.

He looks at me, those ridiculously pale blue eyes of his are unreadable, which catches me off-guard. Since meeting Ax just a short time ago, that feels like forever ago, he always seemed to have a smile. But something was going on with him.

"Are you okay?" I ask.

My gaze runs over his muscled body. I'd never before found a man's thighs and legs sexy, but his are amazing. I don't know if it's the way the firelight seems to warm his skin, casting shadows over his muscles, but I'm transfixed. His cock lays to one side along his leg, big even when unaroused.

I lick my lips and look away from that massive package of his. I had no idea what was going on with Ax, the least I could do was to try not ogle him, even though back at the university I never saw men as beautiful as these guys. It was kind of surreal just sitting next to someone so... beautiful. Like a sculpture.

"I'm okay. It's just..." He frowns and goes back to poking the fire with a stick.

I smile and reach out, unable to help myself. I rub the back of his neck, and he sighs. The tension seems to ease from his body and he drops the stick and lies down, his head on my lap. I continue to stroke his hair, and use my fingers to rub the muscles of his neck and shoulders.

After a little while, he speaks, his voice soft. "I never really told you everything about why I was thrown into the prison."

"Well, you said that you were blamed for killing your wife and her lover."

"Yeah, but there's more."

I don't say anything more, I just keep running my fingers through his hair.

After a minute, he continues. "Shapeshifters are pretty rare. We tend to all live in groups and watch out for each other. For some reason, we have a tendency... to snap. I don't know why, but I suspect it has a lot to do with the way we're raised. Most of the parents in our communities tend to be a little fucked up. They also really encourage us to marry within our own kind, since there's already so few of us."

"Makes sense," I say, my hand runs down his neck and begins to work the knots there again.

He sighs. "It made sense to me too. When my parents invited another family over one night, and they brought their daughter, Olivia, I was barely nineteen. Olivia and I saw each other around, but we'd never really connected. I found her... sort of... not very bright. She was really into her appearance, and she had always seemed more focused on being popular than anything else. In high school, I had a few buddies who I hung out with, but I'd never cared about dances and shit like that, which she was obsessed with. But our parents really pushed it, and after a few months we talked. She said it made sense for us to get married and have shapeshifter kids. I didn't hate her, and it was so important to our community, so we went for it."

It's strange for me to hear him talking about carrying on their powers and things like that. After majoring in English, I'd learned so much about history through literature. The idea of carrying on family lines felt more like something royalty did, not shapeshifter communities. Still, I found it interesting.

"The thing was, we just never felt romantically interested in each other. We didn't even have anything in common. She was a hairdresser who liked to go line dancing and out for drinks with her girlfriends. I was a construction worker who worked long hours. Then, me and my buddies would hit the gym, then get beer, drive our trucks out to the woods, and lie in the back looking at the stars and talking about life. We realized pretty quickly there wasn't anything between us, but we had a house together, and life wasn't bad, so we just kind of did our own thing."

He stops talking, and he rubs his face against my leg through the blanket for a minute. Almost like he needs the comfort of my touch. "She had this client. A regular of hers. When she first told me about him, she seemed a little creeped out by him. As time passed, I found out that he'd started buying her presents, and she'd started to like him. When she told me that they were interested in each other, I was a little surprised. She explained that he was just a little odd, but not a creep. I told her to do whatever made her happy."

"That was... nice of you," I say.

He shrugged. "Olivia wasn't a bad person. I knew eventually we'd get a divorce, and I thought maybe it'd be easier if she'd found someone else. But then," he releases a slow breath. "One day I came home to find our living room covered in blood. The man, James, was a demon. A big time politican. He'd literally ripped her head clean off, then went to work ripping off her limbs, disemboweling her..." He swallowed hard. "I was sort of frozen. I asked him why, and he said that she'd turned him down for sex, and that she was his property. When he'd tried to get what was 'his,' she had slapped him. So, he killed her."

"Oh, Ax..."

"I saw red. I killed him, and I made it slow and painful. I didn't quite remember doing it, but the state of his body told me I had." His voice has taken on a harsh edge. "When the police came, it turned out James wasn't just a politician, he worker with the Enforcers too. No one believed me that James had killed her. They pinned it on me. Olivia's family spat on me and called me a monster. My own family disowned me, and I was taken to Nightmare Penitentiary."

I don't know what to say, but my heart hurts for him. "I'm so sorry."

He closes his eyes, and the muscles in his jaw work. "I just wanted you to know. When things first started between us, I wasn't really thinking about a future. I just wanted to get through each day." His eyes open and lock onto me.

"And even though this situation might be worse than before, I've started imagining a future. With Blade. With Gabriel. And with you. But I knew there couldn't be anything real between us if you didn't know the full truth, and then got to decide if you still wanted to be with me."

The last part surprises me. "Why would I not want to be with you?"

He looks at me as if in disbelief. "I was thrown in prison for the crime of killing my own wife. Most women would hesitate to trust a guy after that."

I shake my head. "Ax, this isn't like the human world. In the human world, people serve jail time for stalking, rape, and murder every day. Any smart woman would take a good long look at any man with a history like that and do some serious research before going anywhere near them, and they should. So many times they seem to think it'll 'never happen to them too,' which is stupid. But in this supernatural world, there's no trial, there's no search for evidence, there's no innocent until proven guilty. Hell, I was thrown in here for 'killing' half a dozen men. Plus, there's the fact that you've proven yourself to be a good person over and over again. Why would I even hesitate to trust you when you've only ever shown me that you can be trusted?"

"You're amazing," he says, his mouth quirking into a smile.

I lean down and kiss him gently. "I know."

He laughs. "So, are you going to tell me more about 'killing half a dozen men'."

I grin. "Well, being the half-human daughter of a wraith has its advantages, but having my body suddenly be taken over and then being dragged to people who are dead and dying... it's one of the disadvantages."

Ax seems to settle in, and I tell him the whole story of being dragged to that park off campus and finding the dead Enforcers. I also remember details I'd almost forgotten, like how it sounded like a woman had been taken out of the Enforcers' custody. But what starts out as a tale of how I ended up in the prisons turns into him asking all sorts of questions about my life, my mom, and even being a teacher's assistant at the college. I'm surprised by how fascinating he seems to find my life.

When I run out of things to say, I grin down at him and kiss him again.

Behind me I hear Blade say, "so your mom doesn't know what happened to you?"

I turn around and find Gabriel and Blade staring at me. My cheeks feel hot, and I try to recall if I said anything that might've been embarrassing in front of a whole audience. "Sorry, did I wake you guys?"

Blade runs a hand through that too-long, tangled blond hair of his. "No, remember that we don't need as much sleep as you do. You, however, should be asleep."

He's probably right. But for some reason, sleep seems less important than bonding with my mysterious men.

Gabriel surprises me by saying. "You'll see your mom again, okay?"

An image of my mom comes to me, and I hate that it's suddenly hard to swallow. Telling Ax about my life had been nice, but now it suddenly felt so bitter-sweet. My mom, my life, all of it felt strangely different viewed from the lens of a person who could never return to that life.

Ax slowly sits up and tucks my hair behind one ear. "Go lay down."

I nod and cling to the blanket that wraps around me. When I go and lie back onto the blankets, Gabriel tugs me against him and wraps an arm around my waist. His warmth is oddly comforting, and I feel my eyelids growing heavy. A slight movement draws my eye to the doorway. I catch Storm disappearing from the room, and my heart hammers. *How much of what we said did he hear?*

And why did I wish he would just stay here with us?

10

STORM

I sit in my hiding place above the demon's tunnels and stare into the darkness. The pillows and blankets that I've formed into a massive nest are usually a source of comfort for me, but now they seem oddly lumpy. Today, I witnessed two surprises. In the past, I had seen the wraith woman die in two different ways in my visions. But she somehow managed to survive both times.

In my long life, I had never experienced anything like a person changing their fate.

And then there had been my response to her and her lovers. I had risked my own life to save the shapeshifter named Ax. It was not something I normally did. Yes, in the past I'd tried to help people, but not at the risk of my own life. Self-preservation was the only thing I had left in this dark prison.

Yet, hearing the stories of the wraith woman and her shapeshifter lover had made me glad that they'd both lived. As far as I knew, very few of the people who lived to reach this area of the prison were innocent. They had to pass a number of challenges to come here, which meant that most of them were both clever and bloodthirsty.

It also made me wonder if they had any chance down here against the others.

The idea disturbed me, and after hours of pondering what this all meant, I came to one conclusion: I would not make it through another round of tests. Whether I lived or died, no longer matter, all that mattered was saving this group of people. They were special, somehow, and I felt that my fate was tied with theirs.

I just didn't know how yet.

But if I wanted them to survive, I needed to step in now, even though I didn't understand everything yet. The next test would come soon. I had no doubt that without me, their chances were close to nothing. What was more, I had survived every obstacle, and yet I'd remained down here. That, along with other small clues, had given me the impression the warden wanted a team to win.

And this time, Elizabeth and her men would become my team.

I rise and dress in my torn jeans. I had many leftover clothes up here from dead contestants, along with many other things I valued. Clothes had never mattered much to me, but I scented jealousy from the other males, so I would tread cautiously around their female.

Crawling through the tunnels, I hesitate at the opening and breath in deeply, scenting for any danger. I can smell the demons at the end of their tunnel, but no one in the open room. So, I jump down, then soundlessly move down the wraith woman's tunnel. When I come to their room, all of them are awake and seated around the fire.

I take a deep breath, and step into the light of the fire.

The dark fae is on his feet in an instant, blocking me

from the woman, and the shifter-vampire is at his side. The shapeshifter rises a little more slowly, one brow lifted in question.

"Hello," I greet.

"What do you want?" The dark fae snarls.

The woman rises and sets a hand on his arm, then she speaks in a gentler tone, "Hi, Storm."

"What's up, buddy?" Ax says, his tone only holding a slight edge.

I meet eyes with the dark fae, knowing that he's the alpha of this group. "I want to help you to survive."

"Sorry, but we don't need your help," he says, too fast.

The woman, Elizabeth, frowns and surprises me by stepping away from the alpha. "Survive how?"

"I want to teach you to hunt the waters for food. I want to teach you the secret places down here. And I want to fight at your side in the competitions."

"And all that out of the kindness of your heart?" The dark fae asks, and again I feel him probing my mind with his powers.

"No."

"Everything comes with a price," the half-breed says. It's not a question, but a statement.

"Then why?" The dark fae asks again.

I hold his gaze. "Your female is important. How... I don't yet know, but I want to find out."

The dark fae seems to swell. "You're not going anywhere near our female."

"*Our* female?" she says, her tone cold. "I don't belong to anyone."

The male's mouth opens in surprise, then closes. "I told you to trust us, that we know better than you."

"And if we had ignored his advice, we would be dead two times over by now," she argues back.

"We don't know him!" The dark fae shouts.

Blade, the vampire, regards me coldly. "We have to be careful."

This... Elizabeth turns her back to me and regards her lovers. "I'm not being stupid here. It doesn't matter why he thinks I'm special, all that matters is that we survive this." Then she looks back at me. "Why do you think I'm so special anyway?"

I tell her honestly. "I have Death Visions. I see people die, over and over again. And nothing ever changes. No matter what I do, they die. For a hundred or more years, I accepted this. Dragged into this prison, I tried again to save people, but it never worked. But you... your death I have seen a million times, but it always changes. I'd thought you weren't real. I had convinced myself that it wasn't possible. But then you came, and I saw you, and you escaped death. Not once. But twice. There *is* something special about you. And I'm tied to you in some way."

"Fuck that," Gabriel snarls.

She lifts a hand, but those blue eyes of hers remain locked on me. "If you betray us, you're going to die. We might not seem dangerous, but we are. Do you understand?"

I nod, and wait.

She turns back to her men. "We're not risking a lot trusting him, not if we're careful still, but we're risking a lot by *not*."

The shapeshifter, Ax, is the first to speak. "As the man whose life he saved, I vote we give him a chance."

Blade speaks slowly next, and I can tell he dislikes me as

he continues to stare. "We can use his help, without trusting him."

"This is ridiculous!" The dark fae says, and I know in that moment he's considering killing me.

"Gabriel, please," she says.

I wait, knowing the alpha will turn her down. Knowing that no matter what the rest of the pack says, he will go with his gut, and that his gut might get him killed.

"Okay," he finally says, "but I'm not turning my back on him."

Surprised, I simply say, "Agreed."

I take a sword with me and lead them to the dark waters. They stand a distance away when I kneel down and wait for the slight flash of silver from the torchlight in the water, then I strike, spearing one of the flesh-eaters. Then, I walk away, careful to never turn my back on the little lake.

"Turning your back will end your life," I tell them carefully.

"Because of the Adaros," Gabriel says.

I nod, impressed. "How did you know?"

"I sensed them," is all he says.

I shudder at the thought of the monstrous beings. "Hunt in pairs. Don't get closer to the water than you have to. And always keep your guard up."

"What are Adaros?" The woman asks.

I look to her dark fae lover, and he finally answers. "You don't want to know, but let's just say they're capable of doing some very awful things. Things you never want to experience."

Her stunning blue eyes widen, and she nods.

After that, they each take a turn catching a fish, and I give instruction when needed. Afterwards, we return to their cave, and Ax begins to cook the fish over the fire. I turn to go when Elizabeth's voice stops me.

"Why don't you join us?"

I look back, feeling uncertain, but Ax grins. "Come on, it's just one meal."

Maybe to them it's just one meal, but to me this feels strangely like the beginning of something.

11

ELIZABETH

Wen we're all finished eating, I sigh and lean back, watching the flames. "I wish we could take a real bath. This whole washing in a bowl thing isn't my favorite."

Storm smiles. "There's actually a way."

He gets up and walks out of the room. When he returns, he has a handful of some of the dried leaves from the wall of sentient beings. "The fish and the Adaros fear the sentient beings. If they even get a whiff of them, they run. In my time here, I throw the leaves in, and the fish and Adaros scatter. I take a bath, then leave. It's perfectly safe."

"That doesn't seem safe," Gabriel argues.

"Come and see then," Storm challenges him.

I get the feeling they're about to argue again, so I stand up. "I'd love to see."

Storm flashes me a small smile, and then begins to lead me from the room. I grab a torch and light it, then keep close to him. A second later, I feel the other guys following us. We enter the room with the lake, and I put the torch in the holder and move as close to the lake as I feel comfortable. To my surprise, Storm takes the torch and leans over the water. Beneath the surface, I can see at least a dozen of those razored tooth fish. It's creepy as hell.

"Whoa," Ax says. "No offense, but I don't think I'm ever getting in there."

Storm smiles, then tosses the leaves in.

I have never seen fish move that fast. One minute they're lazily drifting around, the next they dart for the corner, where there seems to be a deep hole that connects this lake to the main water underground. Storm carefully moves the torch over the water, but it's clear there are no fish left.

He returns the torch to the holder and begins to unbutton his pants.

"I think she's seen enough of your dick," Blade says, an edge to the vampire's voice.

Storm gives a nod, then simply walks into the water, soaking his pants. He folds his legs and leans back, washing his hair and face in the water. For a minute, I'm transfixed by him. He looks like some kind of angel. A glowing, pale shape in the dark waters. My stomach lurches a little, and I remember those damn fish. But Storm surfaces again and stands, then turns as if to show us all he's okay.

"That's good to know for the future," Gabriel says, his voice begrudging. "If we're stuck here much longer, we're going to want to feel clean."

I grin up at him, thankful he seems to be easing up on Storm, but then we hear a small noise that echoes down our tunnels.

"I'll check it out," Storm says, climbing from the water. His jeans drip. Water runs down his massive pecs and stomach, and his pale hair, slicked back from his face, gives him the feel of an ancient god.

"I'll go too," Gabriel tells him. When I look toward the dark fae, I realize he was watching me stare at Storm.

"And I might clean up a bit," Ax says, nodding toward the water. "How long will those leaves work?"

"For quite a while," Storm answers, but his gaze is on the hall.

"Let's head back to our room," Blade says, looking at me.

I nod, and we light a second torch, handing one to Gabriel, and leaving one with Ax, since we have the fire in our room.

Blade is tense as he leads me back to our room, but he relaxes when we're once more sitting by the fire. I sigh and lean my head onto his shoulder. He surprises me by tangling his fingers with mine on my knee.

"We need to talk," he says.

Oh boy, that can't be good. "What's up?"

"Things between us happened so quickly..."

"Yeah." I can feel myself blushing.

"And now I see the way you're looking at Storm."

Fuck, was I really so obvious? "I'm sorry. I swear I'm not usually like this. Yeah, I've always enjoyed sex, but I wasn't this greedy woman who wanted a bunch of dicks in her all the time."

"About that..."

I finally look up at him. His expression is troubled. "What's wrong?"

He releases a slow breath. "You're the mate to my shifter side. For me, there's only you as a female. That's why as much as Gabriel didn't want to share you, he agreed because he knew I didn't have a choice."

It takes me a minute to remember to close my mouth. "What are you talking about?"

"You're my mate," he emphasizes each word.

"Like...?" I feel so dumb.

He sighs. "I always forget how... human you are. A mate is a partner that the wolf inside of me chooses. There's no going back after my wolf chooses. You're my woman from here on out. If I lose you, I could never have another woman."

So many things that I didn't understand suddenly click into place. Not the least of which is the way Blade responded to me when we were locked in that cell together. Just the thought of it makes my nipples harden. I'd thought it was just because he was hurt and needed my blood, but the passionate way he fucked me said it was more than just about blood.

"So, you and Gabriel are comfortable sharing me with Ax?"

He nods. "But I don't know that I could share you with Storm."

I'm suddenly fascinated by my hands. "I never even said-_"

"You didn't have to. I feel something between you, and I'm not going to pretend I'm not jealous. Storm is a full shifter. Some creature that's rare and powerful. And I'm just, this half-breed..."

I look up again, and our eyes lock. For a second, I'm lost in those pale brown eyes of his, then my gaze runs over his too-high cheekbones, and the slight stubble that's begun to grow. "There's nothing about you that you need to be ashamed about."

"You don't understand," he shakes his head, his expression pained. "My mother was a vampire. A shifter... forced himself on her, and I was a product of that monstrous act. Even so, my parents raised me the best they could until one day my mom told me to hide, and a group of shifters came and killed them both. I saw... everything, but I was only seven. I was too scared to do anything to help them. But I knew deep down all of it was my fault. If they'd just chosen not to have me, or given me away, the shifters wouldn't have been able to smell me and track me down to my parent's home. I truly think the only reason they didn't find me that night was because all the blood covered up my scent."

God, these men have been through so damn much. I have no idea how they aren't complete psychos.

"The chief of police found me at the scene. He was a vampire who helped the humans out with supernatural cases. He took me in. He boxed on the side, and taught me to do the same. He was a good man. But outside of him, the vampires didn't see me as one of their own, nor did the shifters. I've had to be careful my entire life, because just my existence pisses both races off."

"Is that why you were thrown into prison? For defending yourself against those jerks?"

He shakes his head and speaks after a long moment. "When I was eighteen, I slowly and carefully went around killing all the shifters who had attacked my parents that night. The supernaturals thought it was some sick serial killer. For a long time no one could figure out who did it, and then... then my father did. He ended up turning me in. He said he'd spent his life trying to turn me into a good man, but that he had failed."

"You wanted justice," I say, some part of me under-standing on a level deep inside. "You didn't get it, so you took it."

"I still don't know if it was right," he tells me softly. "I thought when they were all dead, I'd feel better. But I didn't."

I squeeze his hand. "At least you can move on from all of that."

"Maybe, but I don't know that I can be around a full-shifter. I don't know if I could ever let him get anywhere close to you. He could have any woman. He doesn't need my mate."

I set my head on his shoulder. "I never want to hurt you."

"I know. But you will. Anyone who holds someone else's heart the way you do with mine is bound to hurt the other person."

"I hope not," I say. "But I'm not sure what to do with Storm."

We're quiet for a long time before he speaks again. "See how you feel about him, but I don't want to know about it. And know that I don't think I can accept him."

That seemed like a double-edged sword.

I'm about to ask more when the world suddenly begins to shake. Blade leaps to his feet and helps me up, and then we're both racing down the tunnel. We see all the doors closing. I hear Bron's voice, and then Blade grabs my hand and yanks me back into the room with the fire before the door slides closed too.

My heart's hammering as the rumbling quiets. "What the hell was that?"

Blade's hands are clenched into fists. "Someone sealed all of us into our rooms. We should be ready, just in case."

"In case it's another attack?" I ask, feeling my stomach turn.

He nods slowly and unsheathes his sword.

12

GABRIEL

When Storm and I had come across the new room connected to our main tunnel, we'd entered it cautiously. It was massive, empty, and seemed to split off into two other tunnels. So, we'd cautiously chosen the right tunnel first. I didn't exactly like having Storm at my back, but I was bound and determined to figure him out, and the only way I could see to do that was to spend time with him alone. Because anyone who was looking at Elizabeth the way he did was a threat. Too many times to count the dark fae part of me wanted to end his miserable life. I'd reach for his mind over and over again, but then stop myself.

I didn't trust this man, but if he could help keep Elizabeth safe, I needed to get over myself and let him. Not that allowing him to help meant that I trusted him. It was more that I was willing to *use* him.

Still, it worried me in a strange way that I didn't resort to killing him right away. *Isn't that what I'd done for too many years to count?* My boss gave me a name, and I killed them.

Now a man was treading on my territory, and I hesitated, all for Elizabeth's sake.

I wasn't sure if this change in me was a good or bad thing.

When the right tunnel comes to a dead-end, with half a dozen bodies scattered on the ground, I turn to face Storm. "What the hell do you think this is?"

His pale eyes narrow. "A test. It's always a test."

"How do you know? How long have you been down here?"

He shrugs. "Weeks or months, I can't tell. But before that I was imprisoned for a time too."

"Why?"

Again, he shrugs. "I assumed it was because my kind are rare and highly sought after, but they've never used my gifts to their advantage, so I don't know."

"Your kind?"

He nods, turning around and we start back the way we came, moving slowly and cautiously. "I am an Amorak. My kind comes from the Arctic. We are few, and we do not like to stay together in large packs. And yet, that was our downfall. Our small families were hunted and killed nearly to the point of extinction. Some for our coats. Some taken prisoner for our Death Visions."

"Were you thrown down here with your own kind then?"

He shakes his head. "Just other shifters."

"And what happened to them?"

"They all died," he says, and there's no remorse in his voice.

My teeth clench together. "It sounds like you didn't mind that they died."

He glances back at me. "I see death when I wake. I see death when I sleep. Death has always simply been death.

Yes, sometimes the visions get to me and I try to stop them, but Elizabeth might be the first person I can actually save."

"Is that all she is to you, someone to save?"

He continues walking again. "My wolf likes her. I find her surprisingly attractive. Since the first time I saw her in my visions, I stroked myself thinking of her, but she's even more beautiful in person."

I react without thinking, striking out at his legs with my mind. He falls forward, then growls and looks back at me.

"Don't look at my female," I say, a threat in my words.

"Careful, dark fae, my kind are old. You might not find me so easy a victim."

What the hell does that mean? "And you might find that I'm the person who will finally kill you," I threaten right back.

He climbs to his feet, and his massive body seems to fill the space. We glare at each other, and I'm ready and willing to beat the shit out of him if he ever talks about Elizabeth like that again.

"For a man who's only half dark fae... who cannot see ghosts or speak to monsters, you're cocky."

How does he know that about me?

I take a step closer, careful to conceal my uncertainty. "I don't need to talk to ghosts and monsters, because I have my kind's most useful power."

I'm about to hurt him again, just to prove my point, when I hear the smallest sound somewhere in the darkness ahead of us. Storm must have heard it too, because he whirls around.

From out of the shadows a creature like nothing I've seen before emerges. It's almost human, except naked and emancipated. Its pale shoulders are bent over, and every bone in its body is visible. It's mouth is quirked and stretched in a weird way, and its pupils are red and seem to glow. I've never in my life seen something like that, and I pray to hell that I never do again.

"What the fuck is that?" I whisper, gripping my sword and the torch harder.

"A ghoul," Storm says.

I take a step back, and so does he. Instinctually, I reach for its mind... and feel nothing. It's as if these damn tests have been specifically tailored to prey on our weaknesses. *How the fuck does a dark fae, who can kill with a thought, keep being paired with creatures without minds or souls, or whatever the hell my kind needed unless it was on purpose?*

"So, we just chop off its head?" I ask.

The thing still hasn't moved but it rotates its head to the side in a creepy-as-fuck way and looks at me with those red eyes. Its lips pull back to reveal a row of sharp teeth, and off in the distance I hear the sound of a scream echoing through the tunnels.

"Afraid not," Storm says. "The only time I saw these come after people... they didn't live."

"But there's only one of them," I say, frowning.

"No, there's never just one."

I'm about to argue when twin red eyes appear in the darkness. First one set. Then another. Then another. After a minute, there's easily six sets of eyes.

"Storm? What the fuck is the plan here?"

"Nothing," Storm says softly. "No matter how this goes, we're going to die."

A chill rolls down my spine, and then there's another scream in the distance. *Was that Elizabeth? Are Ax and Blade okay?* But I don't have a chance to think of anything else before the ghouls leap toward us.

13

AX

I'm imprisoned in the room with the lake. My lone torch lighting the darkness. A scream comes every so often from the other side of the wall that blocks me in here, but I can't tell who it is that's screaming, or even if it's a man or woman. I can't imagine there's a good reason we were all sealed into our caverns, except that something bad is going to happen.

So, even though I'm still dripping from the water in the lake, and half dressed, I carry the torch around the room. Checking the shadowed areas for danger. I do one lap, then stare out at the dark waters. Were the leaves Storm threw into the water still working to keep the flesh eaters away? I didn't know, but I sure as hell wasn't about to find out.

Going back to the doorway that's been closed off, I kneel down and try to find any weakness in the wall. My fingers skim the stones, and I look closer, trying to spot anything that might be used to open the door. There aren't any markings, and when I try to shove the wall up, nothing happens. I'm so fixated on the wall that I don't know how long the dripping sound has been there when I hear it.

Every hair on my neck stands on end, and I'm breathing hard as I reach my fingers out for the hilt of my sword. I swear I feel breath on my neck when I whirl around and hold both the torch and the sword out in front of me.

Just a few feet away, a creature unlike anything I've ever imagined stands just in front of the water, it's snakelike tail still dipped into the lake. It stands at easily my height and carries a spear in one hand. Its head is smooth. Its body is scaled. And from the waist up the creature could easily be a bald, strangely handsome, man. Other than the claws on the ends of its hands.

"What do you want?" I whisper, not even sure it has the ability to speak.

It cocks its head. "Want? I want to help you Ax," it says, it's words strangely smooth, so smooth that they seem to echo through my mind.

"You're an Adaro," I say, my pulse picking up. "The thing Storm warned us about."

I swear the creature smiles. "Storm fears the dark truth in his soul. He fears to admit that he is the reason his pack died. But you, Ax, are different. You know that you are not the reason your wife died, but you do want to know the truth of what happened. I can give you that truth."

Fuck. I had tormented myself for far too long about why no one had believed my account of what happened to my wife. For so long it ate at me. It consumed me. I felt like I was losing my mind as I tried to piece together what could have happened, but I'd found some peace in knowing that I would never really know.

But now this fearsome creature seemed to be opening up those old wounds, and I didn't know how to feel.

"You have nothing to fear from me, Ax, and everything to learn."

My grip loosens on my sword and the world around me fades away.

He's right. Isn't he?

I try to recall what I knew about these creatures, but there was nothing in my mind beyond my thirst for the truth. My thoughts outside of that desire for the truth are fuzzy, meaningless, and my body feels strangely light. As if I'm no longer touching the ground. As if I'm no longer... me.

My lips move, even though I don't know what I'm going to say. "Show me," slips from my lips.

14

ELIZABETH

Nothing bad happens. Which should reassure me, but doesn't. I circle the room, thumping the walls, studying the cracks, but find no way to escape. And yet, something crawls beneath my skin. A warning that if we're safe, the others aren't.

"Just sit down, there's nothing we can do."

I whirl and find Blade studying the fire. He's trying like hell to look calm and relaxed, but his hands are curled into fists on his knees. And his leg bounces ever-so-slightly.

"We have to do something! Can you do that thing you did for me... can you reach into their minds?"

Those pale brown eyes of his meet mine. "If they're in danger, I don't want to distract them from it."

"Shit!"

He's right, but I hate that he's right. At any other time, I might think I was overreacting by being so upset, but everything in this damn prison had been trying to kill us since day one. So, I drop to my knees and start to crawl around the room, checking for anything I might have missed.

When I get to the back corner, I freeze. There's a small

hole in the corner. But even as I stare at it, a mouse slowly comes out and stares at me. I stare back at it. There's something far too intelligent in the way it looks at me.

And maybe the guys would think I was a fool, but I set my hand down in front of it. I'm fully prepared for it to bite me when it inches forward and sniffs my fingertips, then continues forward until it sits in my palm. It's whiskers tickle me, and I slowly bring the white mouse to my face, then frown as I see bright red on its fur. Using my other hand, I touch the red, and study my fingers, surprised to find that the scarlet liquid now marrs my fingertips.

I pull my fingers closer and sniff. A coppery scent washes over me, and a shiver moves down my spine. *The red? It's blood.* Of course it's freaking blood.

"There's blood on this mouse," I say.

I feel Blade stirr behind me, and the mouse starts to jerk strangely, so I lower my hand. The little creature jumps out of my palm and dives back into the hole. When Blade stands over me, I show him. He leans down and sniffs the blood, then his eyes darken.

"That's Ax's blood."

I leap to my feet and go back to the stone door, pounding against it. "Ax! Ax!"

Blade's hands grip my shoulders. "Calm down, a little blood doesn't mean anything."

I spin toward him. "Where did we leave him... in the room with the water?"

Every muscle in Blade's body stiffens.

"Is it those damn fish?"

He shakes his head slowly. "Ax is too smart for that. Besides, the mouse wouldn't be alive if it went in that water."

"Then what?"

"The Andros." He moves past me and runs his hands

along the wall until he gets to the bottom. Then, he crams his hands under the stone and strains.

Slowly, painfully slowly, the wall is pulled up. Sweat runs down his face, and the veins on his neck stand out, but at last there's enough room for me to slide under.

So, I do. I slip out into the hall and wait. Blade says, "I can't fucking climb under it!"

And then, the door slams back down. I hear his hands beat against the wall, but I'm in complete darkness now. Carefully, I start down the hall, letting my hand run along the stone. I inch forward, trying to remember how far down the room with the water was.

A strange laugh comes from somewhere around me, and I stiffen. For a minute it's like the voice out of my nightmares, and then I recognize it as the warden. *Is he watching me even now? Or am I just imagining it?*

My foot splashes into something. My heart hammers and I lean down. Stretching out my fingers, I touch the liquid and then bring my fingertips to my nose. *Blood.* Goosebumps erupt on my arms as I reach back down and try to feel where the blood could be coming from. At last I realize that it seems to be leaking from beneath the wall.

And I think I might be outside of the room with the water.

"Ax!" I scream his name. "Ax!" My hands pound on the stone. But no matter how much I try to lift the wall, or find a weakness in it, I find nothing. So, I just keep screaming his name, hoping that when the door opens, I won't find Ax dead on the other side.

15

STORM

Even though I know it's impossible for us to survive the ghouls, I don't have it in me to go down without a fight. I shift into my wolf as the ghouls attack, and I fight right back. But no matter what I do, no matter how many of them I temporarily kill, or how many limbs I tear away, there's always more.

A whimper escapes my mouth as two ghouls bite my back, and I roll free, then dodge backwards. Gabriel is instantly at my side. He swings his sword recklessly in front of him, striking any of the ghouls that get close, but he's continually inching backwards, just as I am.

In the back of my mind, I know this tunnel ends soon. I also suspect the bodies left there were from other prisoners, just like us, who faced these ghouls. In front of us, just at the edge of torch light, I see the ghouls pulling themselves back together. Those eerie lips of theirs parted in a mockery of a smile.

"Fuck," Gabriel mutters beside me as claws catch his arm and tear open his flesh.

Blood drips down and the coppery scent fills my nostrils,

a growl tears from my lips, and claws slash my face, tearing strips into my muzzle. Suddenly, I feel the end of the tunnel close behind us. I chance a look back, and I'm right. We're out of room to run.

Gabriel suddenly says, "cover me, and I think I can save us."

There's the strangest note to his voice. Part of me wants to try darting around the ghouls, to see if I can make a run for it. It's the same instinct that has kept me alive all these years while others failed around me. But the other part of me knows there's nowhere else to go, that Gabriel will die if I do so, and then the ghouls will simply come for me. Or maybe they wouldn't, but for once in my life while the people around me die, I don't want to be the only one to survive.

So, I do as he says. I move to stand in front of him. I flash my teeth and let a growl roll from me that echoes through the hall. The ghouls move forward and I bite, I claw, I fight, but teeth and nails seem to slice into me from every direction. Whimpers escape my throat. I hiss as teeth tear into my shoulder, and then there's a horrifying moment where I'm sure Gabriel found a way to survive and left me here to die.

My legs give out beneath me and the ghouls pile on. The slight light from the torch is blocked out and sharp pain assaults every part of my body until blackness edges my vision. And then something changes, I don't know what.

The weight on top of me fades.

The light from the torch appears again.

I crack my eyes open and look around me. People are fighting the ghouls. Half a dozen people whose movements are strange. People who don't react when the ghouls bite and claw. My thoughts feel fuzzy, and at the back of my mind I'm pretty sure I'm imagining everything in front of me.

"Easy now," I hear someone whisper. Gabriel's face appears before mine, his expression strained.

He works to drag me back against the end of the tunnel. Then, he lies down beside me. I shift back into my human-form and pant, trying to fight through the pain.

"Fuck," he mutters. "You look even worse without the fur."

To my surprise, Gabriel takes off his shirt and begins to shred the fabric. Then, cautiously, he wraps my many wounds. All along I watch him, my thoughts foggy. He has some bloody slashes, the worst of which is on his arm, but he looks pretty damn okay given what we'd been through. Maybe this man was more than just his powers. Someone, somewhere, had taught him how to fight.

He tightens the binding on my shoulder, and I hiss in pain and feel my nails cut into my palms.

"Sorry," he murmurs, and his touch grows softer.

A dark fae who wishes to help me... who tries to be gentle... he is an anomaly.

He keeps wrapping my wounds, and I bite down on my cheek, tasting blood, to keep from crying out. My father had always told me that real men hid their pain. Unfortunately for me, my mother and older sister had said the opposite. When I cried as a child, they were always there with warm hugs and soft touches. They told me that real men weren't afraid to show the way they felt. Even now, I can remember how they smiled down at me, although their faces had been harder and harder to remember as time passed. It was strange how much those memories of my family got me through my pain, but it also meant that there was a weakness inside of me I always had to fight.

I've been hurt. So many many times. I hated it that it was always painful. "No one ever helps me," I say. His gaze meets mine. "Usually I hurt alone."

His gaze tears from mine. "That's how it was before Elizabeth, Ax, and Blade."

I keep watching him as he slowly tends to my wounds.

"Who are those people?"

His hands freeze. Then, slowly, he continues to wrap the worst of my wounds on my shoulder. "They're the dead bodies in the tunnel."

I feel like his words can't be real. "How...?"

"You were right that I'm not a full fae. My father was a necromancer. But my powers... they're hard to work. Usually I only raise the dead accidentally when I'm afraid. But when the ghouls were attacking us, the bodies started to move..."

"A real necromancer," I whisper, wincing as the wound on my shoulder gives a stabbing pain.

It was more than a little bit surprising. Necromancers were rare. Most seemed to live forever, but never had children. The most well-known ones were evil as hell, and had been hunted by nearly every known kind of supernatural.

"What will happen now?" I ask.

He shrugs. "The ghouls will keep fighting. The dead people will keep fighting. But they should keep each other busy until we get out of here. *If* they let us out of here...and when we're safe, I'll pull my powers back, and they'll be bodies once more"

"They will let us out," my head falls back against the stone, and I grit my teeth and force my breathing to remain even. "When enough of us have died."

"Fuck," Gabriel mutters. "I hope Ax, Blade, and Elizabeth will be alright."

I tense and try to sit up.

He shoves me back down with one hand. "There's nowhere to go, so let's stop your bleeding."

"But Elizabeth..."

He looks at me. "She'll be okay."

"I don't even know what she can do. She seems so fragile."

To my surprise, Gabriel smiles. "Elizabeth is many things, but fragile isn't one of them."

Suddenly, the dark fae fades away and a Death Vision strikes me so hard that for a minute I'm lost to the world. I jerk in fear when Gabriel's face comes back into sight, and I know I'm shaking and sweaty.

"What the hell! What was that?"

I must have bitten my tongue, because I taste blood. "A Death Vision."

His eyes hold mine. "Whose?"

I consider not telling him but then decide there's no point. "Ax. Ax is about to die."

Our old house looks exactly the way I remember it as I stand out front and stare at the couple of spots where the off-white paint is peeling. My wife's car is parked in the driveway, and at the end of the cul-de-sac is a strangely out-of-place dark orange truck with rust stains.

"You home early?"

My head jerks to the side. My neighbor, a shapeshifter just like me, is rarely home at the same time I am. Working construction means that I'm usually heading home when the sun sets, and Randal has usually just left for his night shift at the hospital.

I grin. "Yeah, I guess." Although I can't remember why I'm home early.

His mouth pulls into a smile. "Well, say hi to the Mrs. for me."

"Will do," I promise.

He gives another wave, then jumps into his car and drives off. My gaze returns to the house. Something feels... off, but I just can't put my finger on it.

I'm about to head inside when I notice that the trashcan is still at the curb. With a sigh, I grab it, drag it up the driveway, then push open the side gate and roll it to its spot in the backyard. I'm about to head back to the front door when I hear the sounds of raised voices through my open window.

"I'm not in the mood to fuck," my wife's voice is tired.

"Come on, baby. Let me sink my cock into that pussy of yours."

I stiffen. My wife has always had her men on the side. I'm too tired after work to go out looking for other women, but I've never minded. She and I were more like roommates anyway by now. But I've never actually met one of her lovers. If they were just fucking, I'd probably walk away and hang out somewhere until he was gone, but something about the conversation puts me on edge.

"Not right now."

"Didn't you like the necklace I got you?" There's an edge to the question.

"Yeah, but that doesn't mean I have to sleep with you."

"What's that supposed to mean?" His voice is practically a roar.

"Just that! Buying me something doesn't mean I have to sleep with you."

I go to the window and pull myself up onto the air conditioner. I can just barely make them out in the living room. But some muscular guy is sitting next to her on the couch, and there's something in his eyes I don't like.

"You're my woman now, do you understand that? And I can do what I want with you, when I want to!" He stands as he says the words, and his size seems to grow until he triples in size.

Fuck. I jump off the air conditioner and race around to

the backdoor. It's usually unlocked, but when I yank on it, it doesn't open. For a minute my wife stands and glares at him. I can see them shouting at each other, but I can't hear what they're saying, and then I punch through the glass.

The door shatters, but neither looks my way. I can feel my blood pouring out from my hand. I can smell the scent of the coppery substance in the air, and my body seems to ache. But I crunch through the glass, heading straight for them. He reaches out and grabs my wife's arm. I shout in warning, but I can't seem to reach her. He tears off one arm. She screams, and then he goes for the other.

There's so much blood. So much pain. But no matter how hard I run, I don't seem to reach them.

I don't understand. This doesn't explain anything. Somewhere in the back of my mind I'm aware this isn't real. That I lost my wife a long time ago. But I didn't need to hear the argument, I needed to understand why any man would hurt a woman like this. I need to know why no one believed me that day.

"No!" I shout, my heart in my throat. "Stop!"

The vision changes, and I see myself walk into the room. It's strange. I remember exactly how I felt as the beastly man turned around, standing over my wife's dead body. My body had started to swell and grow. His eyes had widened, and he'd charged.

There was no going back then.

The vision changes to one I'm not familiar with. My wife's parents are crying on the couch, and my parents are sitting across from them. My mom and dad keep exchanging looks that don't make sense to me when two people are sobbing just feet away.

My mother-in-law lifts her head, tears stream down her

face. "Do you really think he did it? Do you really think he snapped?"

Snapped. That's how they described it when a shapeshifter went crazy... something that happened far too often in our community. But snapping usually resulted in stupid shit, like broken barstools, a robbery, a high-speed chase. Yeah, there were fights, but it was usually the result of a prick-boss pushing a shapeshifter until they snapped and beat the shit out of them. Or when two shapeshifters fought over a woman they both loved. Not straight-up murder. Crimes of passion and just plain dumb crimes. But not violence against women. That alone was rare, if not entirely unheard of.

My mom hesitated, seeming to consider the question of whether I actually snapped or not carefully, then spoke. "Here's the thing... we've kind of led people to believe that Ax is half-human, half-shapeshifter. Well, he isn't. He's actually two types of supernaturals."

Wait... what?

"When I got pregnant with him, his father and I were, well, we were fighting. There were other men. One was human, who I assumed was his father for a time. And the other was a powerful, rare, and intoxicating man who seduced me. Later on we did a paternity test, and ruled out Frank. We didn't tell anyone that he could be two types of supernaturals, because we knew he'd be treated as an outcast. We just hoped he was half-human."

"Why didn't you tell us this?" My father-in-law said, his question filled with disbelief.

"Ax doesn't even know," she admitted, and my father took her hand and squeezed it.

There was a silence that seemed to go on forever.

"Mixed breeds that come from two supernaturals snap even more often," My mother-in-law said, sitting up taller. "He had to have done it." Then her gaze moved to my parents. "And I'll never forgive you for this."

I'm overwhelmed. No one ever, not in my entire life, implied that I was anything but a half-human. But if I was mixed with two supernaturals, and they told the police, everything suddenly made sense. Shapeshifters snapped, but to kill one's own wife... that seemed like the kind of evil only a person mixed with two supernaturals could do.

At least according to the shapeshifters. Being mixed with a human was more just a half-breed. But being a mix of two supernaturals was something people truly feared. Blade and Gabriel had, however, proved a thousand times over that that was just shit people made up to explain us away. I'd always kind of thought that mixed breeds didn't just snap, they had hard lives, they were treated like crap, and everyone had a limit.

I'd just never known I was one too.

So many questions were finally answered. So much about what happened that day took on a new meaning. Maybe I should've been more upset that I hadn't known the truth about me, but somehow it was easier to stomach the idea that their view of mixed supernaturals was to blame, not that everyone I loved suddenly thought I could hurt someone I cared for.

The Adaro was right. I felt better now that I knew the truth.

Around me, the vision of the people talking fades away, and I'm cold. Terribly cold.

Suddenly, I'm no longer in my parent's house. I'm no longer watching people I'll never see again. I'm staring up at a stone ceiling, and something cold and wet is touching me. I feel blood pouring from my throat, and I shove out. The cold shape flies back, hitting the ground, and I struggle to my feet.

There's a horrible moment where I know the side of my neck has been torn open like some beast was feeding on me, but it's only made worse when I realize I'm sitting in a pool of my own blood. When I look at the scaly creature, it's face covered in blood, it hits me that it was feeding on me.

"You tricked me for my blood!"

His lips quirk into a semi-smile. "No, I tricked you for your soul."

"My soul?" *Fuck*. I *felt* different.

It climbs to its feet, and I mirror its movements, rising to stand too. The ground tilts under my feet, but I lean on the wall to keep from falling.

"Don't you know what an Andros does?" It cocks its head. "We can reveal all the secrets within your soul, but it comes with the price. We take everything good from you until nothing is left but the bad. And then with time you either become something like me... or a ghoul."

"You didn't even reveal anything to me! What am I? A mixed breed? Mixed with what? And I still don't understand how that bastard could kill my wife in cold blood. I have *more* answers than when we made this deal" And then there was the other thing, I would've never made the deal in my right mind in the first place.

It'd done something to me.

His smile widens. "If I had taken everything good from you, you would've finally understood how a man could inflict violence on a woman. You'd become the thing you hate most in this world. You'd become the kind of monster who thrives on the suffering of others."

My heartbeat fills my ears. "I could never be that!"

He points to his belly, and a second later a golden light glows beneath the surface of his skin. "You almost were. I fed on so much of you. So much that you'll never be the same again."

I don't think, I just act. I grab my sword off the ground and leap on top of him, knocking him down. I slice open his belly as he screams, and the golden light explodes out of him.

"You don't know what you've done!" He wails.

I don't hesitate. I slit his throat, and his wailing is silenced.

Panting, I sit back, staring at the dead creature. *Did killing it give me back the pieces he took of me? Or are they gone forever?*

I search within myself, but I don't know. *How can I know if I 've changed deep inside?*

The sword drops from my hand, clattering onto the ground. I stumble back from him. *What if he did take so much of the goodness inside of me that I'm the same man I was before? What if I'm dangerous to the others now?* I clench my hands together. If I showed the slightest sign of being something other than myself, I'd walk away from them. All of them.

I just hoped it never came to that.

Suddenly, I feel a strange shaking. Behind me, the door opens, and Elizabeth is racing in a moment later. She sees me and stops dead in her tracks, looking at the blood that coats me. Her face goes white, and her eyes hold unshed tears.

"Are you okay?"

I'm shaking. "I don't know."

Her arms are around me in an instant, and it's hard to swallow around the lump in my throat. Right now I'm holding the woman I love, but if that thing made me into someone else, could I hurt her one day?

I hold her tighter.

17

ELIZABETH

I hear Gabriel call my name. We grab the torch from the room with the water and start down the hall only to see Gabriel and Storm before us, both bleeding and injured. In an instant, Gabriel grabs me and swings me into his arms. He holds me so tightly for a minute that it's hard to draw in a breath, then he mumbles, "sorry," and lets me go. But still, his hands are on me, his face seeming to memorize my own.

"Is everyone okay?" Blade asks from behind me.

I'm hugging him a second later too, and I whisper in his ear. "There was a dead creature near Ax, and he doesn't seem like himself."

He tenses and whispers back. "Did it look like a scaled human?"

I nod, and his grip tightens around me for the briefest moment before he lets me go. His face is a blank sheet as I study him, but I know something is going on behind his calm surface. Something that worries me. I also know enough to keep this to myself until I can ask him.

We hear sobbing in the distance. We all turn to the sound at once.

"What's that?" Gabriel asks.

Storm's face is hard to read in the torch light as he says, "we weren't the only ones tested."

We carefully make our way down the hall, and I see a doorway I've never seen before. But even as I step toward it, the hall begins to shake and the door closes. I want to know what's inside, but I'm not about to duck in and leave my men behind.

"Any clue what that is?"

"That is a bad place filled with death," Storm says, and his gaze meets and holds Gabriel's.

"Was that where you were trapped?" I ask.

Neither man answers me.

"What happened in there?" I press.

"We got out alive," Storm answers evasively. "Which is better than most."

The quiet sobbing continues, and I make a promise to myself to find out what happened in that room. Even though it seems clear it's pulled the two men together, even if they both look badly injured. We continue down the hall toward the sobbing, and Blade has his arm around Ax, helping him stumble after us.

When we get to the main room with the lone bulb overhead, the elementalists are there. The woman is collapsed over one of her men, the man with pale blond hair. He's covered in blood, and his pale skin looks even paler, but I notice that his chest rises and falls. The other three men have bowed heads as they stand over him, and all of them are in rough shape. Their clothes are singed, torn, and blood has painted their skin red. The female elementalist doesn't look any better...

"What happened?" I ask.

The woman doesn't answer, she just continues to cry.

"An Adaro happened," the man with red hair says, and there's so much anger in the word that it surprises me.

"An Adaro?"

He nods. "He was trapped in the room with the water. The creature came. We don't know what knowledge it offered him, but he must have accepted."

I look at Blade, confused.

Blade responds softly. "Adaros are fallen angels. A rare species that angels don't even want to be associated with. The Adaros fell a long time ago, a special group of them that people know little about. They live in water and suck out all the goodness inside of people, leaving behind a shade of a human. Basically, a creature who is the darkest side of humanity. The people who are attacked by these beings rarely survive. And if they do, most people wish they hadn't."

The crying woman looks up through her tears. "Shut up! Just shut up! We got him out in time! He's still himself."

The red-haired man kneels beside her. "We should take him back to our tunnel and keep him safe."

Demons suddenly stagger out of their tunnel. There are three of the men, and they're covered in blood and opened wounds that are already healing before my eyes. They remind me of the moment after they came back to life.

"Where did they go?" The biggest of the demons hisses.

"Who?" I ask.

"The ghouls," he sneers. "This isn't over yet."

A demon behind him adds, "they killed us, which was to be expected, but when we awakened, Xarron was gone. We don't know what they'll do to him when he comes back to life, but we know it won't be good. Draggos will find him and save him. He always does."

The big demon looks at the man on the floor. "He wasn't attacked by ghouls." He inches closer and inhales sharply.

"He smells of an Adaro." Dragos's voice is dangerously low.

The female elementalist glares at him, but the man with light brown hair steps in front of her and the wounded man. "You take care of your man, we'll take care of ours."

"If he has become a shade, we should kill him now, else unleash something far more dangerous on us all," the big demon hisses, taking another step forward.

Flames leap to life in the red-haired man's hand. "Keep walking and I'll burn off your flesh. You might survive it, demon, but you won't want to.

Draggos opens his mouth to respond when we hear a man's scream. It's a sound of pure terror and pain.

"Xarron!" Draggos says, then turns and races back down his tunnel.

The two twin dark-haired demons follow quickly after.

We look back to the elementalists. Two of the men kneel down, and the woman finally pulls back. The men lift the pale elementalist off the ground, leaving behind a pool of blood. They start back down their tunnel, but the woman pauses and looks back at me.

"They're going to just keep killing us one by one. This isn't a test. It's a game to them. It's a massacre. They're just watching us suffer."

"You don't know that," I tell her.

"Why do you think they marked us?"

I glance at the tattoo on my arm and shiver. Of course, there had to be a more sinister reason for the marking. Why hadn't I thought more about it?

My gaze goes back to her. "We just have to keep going."

Her eyes are stony, even while tears roll down her face. "None of us are getting out of this alive."

And then, she turns and walks away, disappearing into the darkness.

I look at Storm. "Could that be possible?"

He seems unsure for the first time since I've met him. "It could be."

Out of the darkness the three remaining vampires emerge. They look like hell. Their skin hangs strangely, and they have too many wounds, but they don't leak blood. The first of them licks his lips and looks at our group.

Gabriel steps forward and lifts a hand toward him. A second later, he gasps and grabs his head, falling to his knees. But it's only a second, and then he looks up at Gabriel with shocked eyes.

My dark fae smiles, a cruel smile that makes my nipples harden. "Don't even think about it, or I'll kill all of you."

His two friends help him rise. They all look uncertain.

"What should we do?" One whispers.

"Find a weaker prey," he says back, then pushes away from them, and they all head down the tunnel to the elementalists.

That can't be good...

"What was that about?" I ask, confused.

Blade is the one to answer. "They're low on blood. If they don't get more, they won't be able to continue fighting."

I take a step in the direction they'd gone, but Gabriel's hand catches my arm, preventing me from following them. "We have to warn them!" I say, glaring at him.

All my men stare back at me, unmoving.

"Guys!"

"We're weak. We need to heal. Not take on a battle that may weaken us to the point of being deadly," Storm says.

For the first time I'm irritated when Gabriel nods in agreement. "If the elementalists can't handle three wounded vampires, they won't survive here."

"So what... we just let them get hurt?"

"I think they can handle themselves," Blade says, shrugging.

My teeth grit together and I turn and yell toward their tunnel, "elementalists, the vampires are coming to feed on you!"

I hear someone down their tunnel say, "fuck," but I don't know if it's a vampire or an elementalists.

"Come on," Gabriel says, "there's nothing more we can do right now."

I disagree, but there's also the small voice in the back of my head that says survival is more important than anything else, and that we have to take care of ourselves. And yet as we start back to our home in this dark place, another voice whispers that if I keep going down this path, I won't like the person I become.

18

BLADE

S torm helps us catch more fish, and I feel pissed as hell. Yes, we needed to eat. Yes, Ax was in too rough of shape to hunt and had almost instantly fallen asleep. But I didn't want or need Storm's help. I especially didn't appreciate the fact that Gabriel seemed to be buddies with him now. I could feel my fangs elongated in my mouth as my rage seemed to swell inside of me.

When Storm and Gabriel had returned with the food and started cooking over the fire, my hands had curled into fists. I had no doubt if I was a dark fae, I would've killed this shifter. But then again, the shifter half of me wouldn't be raging inside about him being in our territory. The shifter part of me wouldn't have been losing control every time Storm looked at or spoke to Elizabeth.

Finally, I stand, and all eyes are on me. "I need some air."

I grab one of the torches and march down the hall until I come to a stop at a random place. Sliding my torch into a holder, I slam my fist into the stone wall. It's a moronic thing to do. My fist hurts like hell and the stone sits undisturbed, but I don't know what else to do.

"Blade?"

I stiffen. From out of the darkness, Elizabeth emerges, and it's like I'm frozen for a moment. Her beauty is untouched by any female I've seen before. I've never thought much about red hair, dark hair, or blonde hair, but now her fiery locks are as beloved to me as the perfect lines of her face. Those blue eyes of hers lock onto me, and worry makes her nibble her bottom lip.

"Are you okay?" she asks again.

"Are you my mate?" I throw the question at her, needing the answer.

"Blade--"

"Are you my mate?" I demand again.

She moves closer to me, but when she tries to touch me, I step out of reach. I need to hear her words. I need to stop feeling this anxiety inside of me that the full-blooded shifter will simply claim her and take her from me. All my logic whispers that that's what will happen. That now that she's faced with someone better than me, she'll turn away, and I'll die inside.

"Blade. I love you."

I stiffen, glad, but still waiting.

"I don't understand a lot about mates, but you know that Gabriel and Ax are important to me too--"

"And Storm," I add, my blood racing.

"Maybe."

There's a roar that seems to fill my ears. "So you're not mine?"

"I am yours," she tells me. "Always."

I pull her against me, and I know I'm holding her too tightly. "If he joins us, I need it to be my decision too. I can't just see you with him."

"Okay," she says, her words soft. Then she leans up. "If I fuck him, it'll be with your permission."

"I'll claim you as my own. He'll have what I allow," I growl, heart racing.

She strokes my arm, and something inside of me crumbles.

"Do you want him inside of you?"

"I want you inside of me," she says, and each word she speaks sends arousal curling through me.

My body hums for her. Aches for her. My gaze slides over her body, and my resolve crumbles.

This isn't the time.

This isn't the place.

But hell, I need my mate. I need to touch her until this jealousy eases inside of me. Until I can imagine a world where I could be the one in charge of anything that happens between her and Storm.

I undress her slowly, devouring the sight of her body as each article of clothing drops to the ground. By the time she's standing in front of me naked, I'm shaking with need. Unable to help myself, I slide the back of my hand from the space between her breasts down to her belly. Her heated gaze is locked on my hand, and I slide it down further and stroke her. A growl slips from my lips when I feel her wet and eager for me.

It takes all my control to stop touching her and strip for her. But I need to be inside of her, and I don't want anything between us. I like the way her eyes follow my every movement, when her tongue darts out to lick her lips. Yes, I wanted her, but I needed her to want me too. My heart sings when her gaze clings to my hard cock. Her tongue darts out again, and my balls tighten.

Gripping my length, I look at her. "Suck me."

My naked, beautiful mate collapses to her knees and takes me into her mouth. I watch, transfixed by how she sucks my head, then licks the tip. Her breasts bounce a little as she slides further and further down my length, and I groan, releasing my erection and letting her take complete control.

A slight scent catches my attention, and I look out into the darkness. Storm emerges on the very edge of the torch light, and I don't know if it's the shifter within me, or my own twisted mind, but I like him watching. I want him to see that she's mine, not his.

I hold his gaze as I slide my fingers into her hair, and tangle the strands, then grab hard and thrust into her mouth. She moans around my cock, and I'm sure my tip is flowing with precum. My body trembles and I continue to thrust in and out of her mouth harder and harder. She hums around my length, and I jerk, almost spilling my seed right there.

Instead, I pull her back from my cock, then look down at her on her knees. Naked. Submissive.

"Spread your legs further apart," I order.

I feel her shudder and she does as I tell her.

Reaching down, I pinch her nipples, and she gasps. I play with them, holding her breasts, stroking the tips. Hard one minute, gentle the next. And then, I reach between her legs and stroke her pussy, glad to find it soaking, just for me. She breathes my name and wraps herself around my arm as I work her faster and faster. She grinds herself against me, and then one of her hands reaches out to stroke my cock in unison with how I'm stroking her.

I almost come again, but push away from her.

She continues kneeling in front of me, and God do I like the sight of her like this.

Without speaking, I lift her and then push her against the wall. She plants her hands on the stone, and spreads her legs, waiting. I come up behind her and smack that ass of hers, watching as her cheek pinkens. I slap her again and again until she's moaning and wiggling.

Then, I grab her hips, forcing her ass out further. Her hands slide down the wall until she's almost completely bent over. Positioning my cock at her entrance, I don't give her a warning, I just slam in.

She shouts my name, and I fuck her harder and harder.

When I find my rhythm, I grab one of her breasts roughly, and with my other hand, I slide my fingers into her pussy, playing with her clit. She screams and jerks as I rub her clit, making her juices flow. And a second later I feel her orgasm, her muscles squeezing around me in a way that makes every hair on my body stand on end. It feels like her fucking pussy is trying to milk me of my seed, but I just keep slamming into her, faster and faster until I feel her second orgasm hit. Finally, I can't take it anymore; I come, filling her. My head spins, and I'm not satisfied until my hot seed coats her inside, then, at last, I slow my pumping, until she's drained me of every last drop.

"Oh, fuck, Blade, that was so good."

"Am I your mate?" I ask again.

"Yes," she purrs.

I meet Storm's gaze, but to my surprise, he doesn't look angry or jealous. Instead, he strokes his own cock.

In that moment, I realize that I'm the alpha with my female. He's no more than a beta, wishing he could be *me*. In all my time among shifters, there was never anything I had that they wanted. Never.

It hits me that I'm no longer a boy. I'm a *man*. And *I* decide how things will be.

I pull out of Elizabeth. Pressing her against the wall once more, but this time with her back to the stone, I kiss her over and over again, deepening our kiss each time until our tongues are tangling together.

When I pull back, I'm hard again. "You really want Storm too?"

"Only if you're okay with it," she pants.

"Come here," I say to the shadows.

Storm slowly makes his way closer, and Elizabeth gasps at the sight of him.

"You really want this?" I whisper to her.

She nods, her gaze going to his hand fisted around his cock.

"You can have him only the way I say," I whisper into her ear.

She nods without hesitation.

I look at Storm again. "Come taste my mate's lips."

He hesitates, but then moves forward.

I continue to hold her as he leans forward. His first kiss is gentle on her lips, but then he seems to grow more and more needy as he kisses her harder, and I can see their tongues dancing together. The sight of it is arousing. So arousing that it actually takes me by surprise. I'd wanted to see them kiss to be sure of my emotions. I imagined at best it wouldn't irritate me.

But to turn me on...

"Enough," I say, panting, shocked by how much it arouses me to see her touching him.

I pull her away from the wall and Storm, so that her back is against me. My length presses between her lips, and I rub myself in her juices as she shudders.

"Come try my mate's breasts."

This time, Storm doesn't hesitate, he rushes forward,

and his head lowers. His mouth closes around one nipple and he sucks as she gasps and digs her hands into his hair. Her head goes back and he moves to the other breast. I swear this man could suck her tits forever. He cups them, his hands claiming her as his own as his tongue flicks over her hard peeks, and his mouth sucks her deeply into his mouth.

"Oh, fuck," she groans. "Fuck. Fuck me. God damn it, fuck me."

That's exactly what we need to do.

"Stop," I tell Storm.

His pale eyes seem to darken, and he takes a step back.

I hold his gaze as I lift her under her thighs and keep her against my chest. I change the angle of my cock to slip into her ass. She cries out, and I push myself inch by inch deeper. I don't even think Storm is aware of it when he kneels down to watch my cock sinking deeper, but he grabs a hold of himself and strokes himself faster and faster.

When I reach my hilt, Elizabeth's arms come around my neck, and I know she's on display for this shifter. I start to fuck her in the ass, hard as hell, and her breast bounce. She drips with desire, and Storm's expression is fierce as he watches it all unfold.

At last, I say, "shifter, want to try my mate's pussy?"

He stumbles to his feet and comes toward us. For a moment he doesn't seem to know what to do, but then he grabs her hips and eases his big cock into her pussy. Elizabeth thrashes between us, moaning my name first, and then his. Within seconds, he's fully inside of her, and then we begin to fuck her together. And this, this moment, it feels right. Pack members rarely share a mate, but this feels natural down to my soul. He begins to kiss her again, and then I sink my aching teeth into her throat and start to drink my sweet mate's blood.

When she orgasms around us, we come almost as one, filling her up in all ways with our needs.

It takes a long time. It seems we have a lifetime of cum to release into this sweet woman, but at last we're gasping together. And the world around us is silent. I pull my teeth from her neck and feel content down to my very soul.

"Well, fuck."

I turn and see Gabriel and Ax watching us.

"So I guess you guys made up?" Ax asks, lifting a brow.

I look at Storm. "She's my mate."

He nods.

Elizabeth sighs between us. "I don't care what you call me, as long as we do that again."

The men surprise me by chuckling.

After a minute, Gabriel says, "we should clean up and rest."

He's right, but my cock still longs to take my mate again.

19

ELIZABETH

We're all fully clothed and eating around the fire. No one says much, but every time I look up, at least a couple of sets of eyes are on me. I try to keep my eyes on the fish on a stick in my hand as I pull off flakes of meat, eating slowly, and letting my mind wander. Everything seems to happen so fast in these prisons, and I'm finding it hard to explain, even to myself, what I'm doing. My gut feels like I know and trust these men more than anyone I've met in my life, but my head keeps saying that I'm still just getting to know them.

And, of course, I'd already slept with all of them.

It was just so bizarre. Blade had gotten me so hot and horny. At first, I'd just thought all his talk about Storm was just to turn me on. But when he'd invited the big shifter to join us, it'd felt like a fantasy coming to life. Even when he'd started kissing me and touching me, I figured Blade would stop things before they went too far.

And then they'd both fucked me. Penetrated me at the same time. Left me begging and gasping between them while my body heated with desire. Just the thought of it made me tremble.

"Does she do this a lot?" Storm asks, a curious note to his voice.

"Yeah," Blade says, not looking up.

"Do what?" I look between them, confused.

Storm's pale eyes lock onto mine. "You were just fucked by two healthy males, and yet I can smell desire coming from you still."

I feel my cheeks heat. I open my mouth to speak, but no words come out.

"She's lucky there's four of us," Ax says, his tone nonchalant. "She might have drained you two, but Gabriel and I should be more than good to go after dinner."

"Do Blade and I not get to pleasure ourselves with her again then?" Storm asks, frowning.

"Guys!"

They all look at me.

"I'm... uh... not an object. I get a say in this too."

They all laugh as one, and my cheeks feel like they're on fire.

Ax takes my hand in his, and our eyes meet. "Of course you get a say in this. Hell, you're the one running the show."

I can't help but smile back. "Just wanted to make sure."

Suddenly, a loud blaring sounds, and we all turn to look at the entrance to our little room. The sound grows in volume until I have to press my hands to my ears. Storm stands and gestures at our weapons and the door. Each of us grabs a sword, and I put a couple daggers in the sheath around my waist. We follow Storm out into the dark hallway, but luckily, Ax grabs a torch. We head down the hallway until we reach the main room with the one lone bulb. Everyone gathers, including the group of elemental-ists, who carry the unconscious man with pale hair between them.

"What's going on?" she shouts.

No one answers, but Storm's hands are curled into fists.

The doors to the tunnels suddenly slam shut, and we're all sealed into the one room together. The ceiling opens up above us and smoke pours down. I squint, grasping my blade tightly. I barely make out the men in black outfits that drop down into the room, but I do, and my stomach twists. I glance at my men to warn them, but the smoke is so thick already that I can barely make out their shapes.

Storm's voice comes in my mind. *Careful, there are enemies among us. But if we aren't careful, we may harm each other.*

I hear someone scream and the sounds of swords strik-ing. Heart racing, I move until my back hits the wall, and I wait, sword trembling in front of me. Only, I spot the flick-ering of the bulb above me, and my stomach twists. *No, no, not right now. I can't...*

But already I can feel my body tensing. My legs and arms no longer obey me, and my sword tumbles from my fingers onto the ground. I want to cry out, to tell the guys, but I'm afraid that speaking will only bring our enemies to me.

My feet start carrying me forward. All around me shapes fight. Sparks fly from swords clanging against swords, and I see a spark from a dagger striking a wall. But even though I'm recklessly walking through a battlefield, I can't convince my body to obey me. Slowly, I come to one corner.

Kneeling down, I spot one of the vampires. Blood pours from his lips, and his eyes are wild. I want to move now. I want to run. But even as his eyes meet mine, a sword plunges into his throat, and I watch him die. His soul seems to glow as it leaves his body, and then it slams into me with all the force of a brick wall.

I collapse back, breathing hard, knowing that I should finally be able to leave now, but I don't know if I'm safer here or out on the battlefield. A shape is suddenly looming above me. One of the men in black, and I swear his lips pull back into a smile. I lift my hands and will my powers to obey me. To save me. The man flies backwards, and I can just barely see him as he explodes, then is swallowed by the smoke.

Standing, a tremble wracks my body. My powers flow through me, strong after absorbing the soul of the vampire. I hear Gabriel yell my name. I don't respond. I lift my hands to the air as another scream tears through the space. I focus on the smoke, and it lifts as if gravity has changed. It lifts higher and higher until it fades from the room. When I look around, I see two demons fighting each other. Two dead demons. And one vampire has plunged his sword into the belly of another.

None of the men in black are alive any longer.

"No!" The vampire says, as his brother crumbles to his knees.

His face is a mask of horror. His hands shake. He crumbles to his knees, and his injured brother is staring at him with wide eyes. Carefully, he pulls the sword out of his brother's belly, and blood pours out. The injured man tumbles over, and he removes his shirt and presses it to his brother's stomach. His eyes are wild as he looks at all of us.

"I thought he was an enemy!" He sounds desperate.

It's strange. After everything we'd been through, after everything the warden did to us prisoners here, it was this twisted shit that really fucked with us.

"That was the trick," Storm says, softly. "Not to just kill easy opponents, but to confuse us enough to hurt each other."

The room is silent.

"Those fucking bastards!" The female elementalist screams. "Isn't it enough we're imprisoned for false reasons? Isn't it enough that we've survived this far? They have to keep torturing us?"

The room shakes and the walls lift to reveal our tunnels once more.

I look at the female elementalist. Two of her men are badly injured, the pale one from before is still unconscious, and the red-haired man stands over her and the other men, looking angry. But I don't blame them. It seems this place is hell-bent on taking us down one after another.

The two demons on the floor start to twitch, and they sit up with a gasp of breath.

One of them looks around and a string of curses explodes from his lips. "First the fucking ghouls kill me and then guards!"

Daggos, the largest demon scoffs. "Forget it, brother, you were still weak." Then he offers both the demons his hands and helps them to their feet. Then all four of the demons are standing in a ragged group, glaring at us.

"Clear the arena," the warden's voice says over the speaker, still garbled, but clearly him.

I go to my men. The demons shoot us all another dirty look and go down their tunnel, and the vampire wraps an arm around his injured brother and begins to drag him away.

"We need to go," Storm says.

I nod, and we head toward our tunnel. But I pause when I realize the elementalists aren't going.

"We have to get out of this area," I tell the woman, as Blade tugs at my arm.

Tears race down her face as she looks back at me. "No. I'm done with their games. If they're going to kill me no matter what, I'd rather die with my men."

I try to take a step closer to her, but Blade's hand closes around my arm and starts hauling me down our tunnel.

Storm says behind me, "they'll poison the room. Anyone remaining will die."

Blade seems to pull me harder until I'm almost out of the room.

"Did you hear what he said? They'll poison all of you. You're just going to die if you stay here!"

Her face is pained, and she seems to stare at nothing at all.

I reach for her. "Come on! Get up! Don't let them break you!"

Her man kneels at her side. The injured men don't speak.

I look back at my men. "We have to help them. To force them to see reason!"

They're a sea of stoic faces.

Gabriel tells me, "they're making their choice. We need to make ours."

I shake my head, then shout at her again. "Get up! You're letting them win!"

Suddenly, she seems to snap, and her expression is furious. "I attacked my own men! Don't you get it? They confused us! I hurt them, and I didn't even know it!"

I'm suddenly tossed over someone's shoulder and we're headed down the hall. My shock fades, and I kick at whoever is holding me and reach for the woman. "They tricked you! It wasn't your fault! Get up! Get to your tunnels!"

"It's over," she says, and another tear rolls down her face.

Our eyes lock as the door to our tunnel begins to close. I scream. I fight the person carrying me, and I beg her to run with her men before the doors close. I beg until I'm sobbing. But her eyes simply hold mine until the doors seal shut.

I'm put down onto my feet by the fire in our room, and I react without thinking, slapping Gabriel. He doesn't look surprised or even hurt, so I slap him again and again until i collapse into him, and he holds me close, whispering comforting words. Over and over again I see her tear-streaked face and her eyes filled with pain. I can feel deep inside of me what it would be like to be sitting with three gravely injured men I care for and feel like there was no reason left to fight.

But there was. There always was. No matter how bleak, we had to keep fighting, because the alternative was so much worse.

All my men are silent, and my tears start to ebb, I tell Gabriel softly, "I'm tired."

He lays me down on the blankets and wraps himself around me, his touch more comforting than anything that any of them could say or do.

I close my eyes. "I'm sorry I hit you."

"I'm sorry you had to see that," he whispers back.

I'm shocked how quickly I fall asleep, but I swear that I keep crying, even while I sleep. Picturing the woman. Picturing her men. And a tiny voice whispers in the back of my mind that it was luck that Storm had warned us about the trick.

My dreams are filled with a room being filled with a

green gas and a woman holding hands with her men as death closes in around them. I hear her gasping breaths. I see her eyes widen as she realizes she's dying, and then everything goes dark.

20

GABRIEL

We sit together as a group around the fire later. I've wrapped Elizabeth in blankets, but even though she sleeps, she continues to weep. It breaks my heart. I've seen so much pain and so much death that it was easy not to fight for people who wouldn't fight for themselves. But for Elizabeth, she was willing to risk her life for people she didn't even know.

It was one of the many things that made her special.

Storm had caught fish with Ax, and the two were sitting close. Ax made a joke, and Storm gave a small smile. For some reason, it made me tense. Before fighting with Storm at my back, I would've killed him for fucking Elizabeth, but something had changed between us.

But we still didn't *know* him. Not really.

My thoughts go back to when I'd raised the dead and when they had fought the ghouls for us. Storm and I had gone back to the door and waited for it to open. In the distance, we could hear the undead and the ghouls fighting, but I also knew it would last as long as I kept them animated, since none of them could die.

And even though my father had been a necromancer, and it had not been the first time I'd raised the dead, it was the first time I'd done it intentionally. It felt strange. I could sense the creatures I'd raised like an extension of myself, and I wasn't sure I liked it.

"So you're half-necromancer?" Storm had asked.

My hands had curled into fists. "What's it to you? I saved our lives, didn't I?"

He'd responded calmly. "Your people are like mine, rare and hunted to near extinction."

I'd look at him, surprised. No one had ever accepted the necromancer part of myself except for Blade, Ax, and Elizabeth. I didn't trust this guy. Trust was earned, not given, but it made me feel strange that he accepted me so easily. *He did understand that I'm the worst mix of creatures, didn't he?*

"It must have been hard as a child to be a dark fae and a necromancer."

I say nothing. *What can I say?*

He continues. "My childhood was lonely. Just my father, mother, sister, and I. We traded with other packs, but our interactions were short and polite. Then we'd return to our cabin in the wilds, snow all around us, and live as if the world outside didn't exist."

"So what happened?" I asked, that seemed about as far from here as I could imagine.

He sounded tired. "One day my father did not return from hunting. I went out to find him. I found his body, and when I returned home, I found the bodies of my sister and mother. I realized then that I should've never let him hunt alone, nor leave my sister and mother alone when I went to search for him. I had condemned everyone in my family with my stupidity.

I ran then, and lived off the lands, but all the time I

could feel that I was being hunted. Why? I didn't know. My suspicion was that one of my family members would have seen an important Death Vision. Something that someone wanted to keep quiet, and they'd used magic to discover such a thing. It was the only possibility in my mind. Most of the people that hunted us wanted us alive. But as I ran from the people shadowing me, tired and hungry, I came to another group that tracked my kind. They took me, and the rest is history."

It was rare I felt sorry for anyone, but I felt sorry for Storm. He wasn't so different from Ax, Blade, and I. We'd all been alone for most of our lives. We'd all suffered great losses.

"Elizabeth isn't like other women," I blurted out.

His icy pale eyes fell on me, but he said nothing else.

"She is beauty in a world of darkness. She needs to be kept safe, but also learn to protect herself, without being broken."

Storm nodded. "If there's anything in this world I won't allow, it's for her to be broken."

When we'd left that room, my anger seemed to be left behind too. It wasn't that I entirely trusted Storm, but I did believe he felt something real and deep for Elizabeth. And I knew what that was like. I hadn't decided how I felt about Storm, but I knew that he could help keep Elizabeth safe.

And then when I'd seen Blade and Storm fucking Elizabeth, I'd been surprised yet again that I hadn't felt jealous. I'd felt aroused. I'd liked seeing the big shifter taking Elizabeth like that. And the moment seemed to connect all of us on a deeper level, which meant, I hoped, that he'd be even more eager to help her survive this.

I'd told myself that was all that mattered.

But as I watch Ax talking to him, and Storm relaxing, it

occurs to me that Ax, Blade, and Elizabeth were my family now. And as much as my instincts were telling me that Storm was different from the other people I'd met, I knew it was my job to keep an eye on him.

Storm's gaze suddenly meets mine. "Are you alright?"

I stiffen. "I'm always alright."

"You had to carry Elizabeth away. She needed to stay safe. I would've done the same if you hadn't."

Holy hell, the weight that seemed to fade from my chest surprised me. With Ax and Blade, they felt like brothers. But even though Storm looked around our ages, talking to him was like talking to a father-figure. *How have I not realized it until now? And why did it feel so damn good to not have the weight of the world on my shoulders?*

Storm looks at Elizabeth. "She'll be fine. All things heal with time."

I just hoped he was right. If we survived all of this, I had no doubt we'd all change, but I didn't want us to lose the parts of ourselves that were important.

21

ELIZABETH

I'm feeling a little better when I wake. We eat more fish around the fire, and everyone keeps the conversation pretty light. I'm actually glad. Somehow, I'm both angry at myself for not doing more for the elementalists, and angry with myself for hitting Gabriel. I know in my heart he was only trying to help, but all these days of tests and fear were starting to wear on me.

Storm stops eating first and sets his food down before stapling his hands in front of himself. The energy in the room changes, and for some reason, we're all looking at him. When our eyes meet, there's the strangest moment of heat between us. It's like as much as my mind has been circling since the tests yesterday, my body still remembers what happened between Storm and I, and that we hadn't discussed it.

"We need to talk," he says.

"Okay." I feel awkward. *Was this about the tests, the elementalists, or the sex?* I wasn't sure I was ready to discuss any of it.

"If the tests go the way they have gone in the past, the next test will be our last."

His words seem to linger in the air.

"Is that... a good thing?" Ax asks.

Storm's gaze darkens. "I've been the only one to survive each of these tests."

"Fuck," Blade mutters.

Storm continues. "There are two vampires left, both of whom are in terrible condition. If they don't find someone to feed off of soon, they're likely to lose entirely."

"So, they're not a threat," Gabriel says, and I can practically hear his brain working.

"I haven't... seen the elementalists bodies yet, but I have no doubt they're gone now," Storm continues.

Ax gives me a gentle look, and I nod back at him to reassure him that I'm fine.

Storm continues. "Four demons are still alive, and with the way they heal, all four are likely in as good condition as we are right now. So, it'll be between them and us."

"Those are good odds," Gabriel says, that hard look coming over his face.

Storm releases a slow breath. "I think if we go against them, you will lose."

"Don't you mean *we'll* lose?" Blade says, and there's an edge to his words. "Or will you abandon us and let yourself win like every other time?"

"That's not how it's gone," Storm shoots back. "I'll fight with you, but depending on the test, we likely won't all make it."

"Like hell," Gabriel says. "You have no idea what we're capable of."

Storm glances at me. "I was impressed to see the wraith

woman use her powers, as well as, well, all of yours. You're a group of rare and strong supernaturals."

I stiffen. "How do you know what I am?"

He doesn't answer.

"I think the shifter likes to spy," Blade says, and his words hold a threat.

My heart races and I hold Storm's gaze. "I don't care that you know, but we can't talk about it. Okay? Wraiths aren't supposed to have children. If anyone finds out--"

"I understand," he says, cutting me off.

Blade drops his food and rolls his shoulders. "So basically, Storm thinks we're going to be dying soon."

Storm gives a sigh, like he's dealing with really irritable children, and continues, "no, what I was trying to say is that I'm not sure we can take on the demons and win. But I think I've found a loophole. Or, more so, a possible escape. It isn't guaranteed. We won't be able to investigate it before the moment, so we could just be trapped, or worse, but I think our chances of survival are better if we do this."

"What are you talking about?" Gabriel asks, frowning.

"During the last test, I noticed that when the walls opened the stone shifts in many places. I already know there are levels above this one, but none of them have led to anything but dead ends. But when I looked up after Elizabeth cleared the smoke, I saw new openings that were never there before. I think if the next time a new room opens, we go up into the tunnels above these we have a chance of finding a way out."

"Or of getting trapped in the room like the elementalists and being poisoned," Blade argues.

"Or we try it and don't have to fight the fucking demons who won't die," Ax counters.

Gabriel is silent but looks pissed.

So, I guess whatever truce we have is gone already. Figures.

I look at Storm, trying to stay neutral. "When you saw these new openings, did they seem to lead to tunnels higher than the ones you've explored?"

He shakes his head. "I couldn't see well enough to be sure."

"So, it could be nothing," Blade grumbles.

"Or a way to escape again!" Ax says, grinning and bumping Blade's shoulder.

"Because the first time went so well." Blade gives him a look like he thinks he's a moron.

Ax gestures with his hand as if to say, forget all about that.

"And do you have any idea what the last test will be?" I ask Storm.

He's quiet for a minute. "The last test is always the worst. The first person to escape, reach the end, or complete the goal, lives. Everyone else dies, one way or another. Even at the best ones, I was in pretty rough shape afterwards. I always needed at least a few days of barely moving to recover... and then more prisoners are dropped down here."

"So... even if we win, we might just have to do this over and over again?"

He nods, then hesitates. "However, I have gathered that they want a team to win. I've wondered if this thing would end if it was more than just me who lived."

Gabriel finally speaks. "I'm not willing to die like a mouse in the ceiling, poisoned by the warden and his assholes. If I'm going to go out, I want it to be fighting. And if we win and are still trapped down here, then we can try simply escaping."

Storm frowns. "I think that's the wrong choice. You have

never been through these tests until the end. You have no idea how dangerous they can be."

"Trust me, I have an idea," Gabriel says dryly.

The big shifter looks frustrated. "Think of Elizabeth. She isn't the strongest supernatural. Perhaps a dark fae will survive, but will a... will she?"

"Don't pretend we aren't *always* thinking of her?" Blade says, and his hands curling into fists.

"At worst case, I'll just kill the demons," Gabriel says, with a wave of his hand. "They might come back, but it'll buy us time."

"And what if they aren't the ones we're fighting?" Storm counters.

Gabriel stands. "I've made my choice. We fight, not hide in the shadows like cowards."

Blade is quick to add. "That's my vote too."

They both look at Ax and I. Ax sheepishly looks at his hands.

I stare at all of them. "I don't know. I have to think."

Blade's dark eyes seem to fill with anger. "You don't need to think. You need to side with the men who have protected you through thick and thin. Men who got you out of the prison safely. Because without us, you'd be dead."

I stand. "You think I don't know that? You think I don't know everything you've done for me?'

He squares off with me on the other side of the fire. "You fucked Storm one time and forgot your loyalties."

His words feel like a blow. I step back, startled.

Ax stands too, his palms stretching out to each of us. "Whoa, whoa, Blade didn't mean it like that. He sometimes says things in the worst damn way."

"That's exactly what I meant!" Blade shouts. "So what's

your choice, Elizabeth? Him or us? Because that's what it was always going to come down to."

I shake my head. "I'm not doing this. I'm not playing your game. I don't have to choose one of you or the other."

"Yes, you do!" His infuriated gazes swing from Storm and I.

I open my mouth, about to say something I know I'll regret. Instead, I spin on my heel and walk right out, grabbing a torch as I go. Behind me, Gabriel and Ax shout my name, but I know I need to walk away. I know that if I stay in that room, I'll say something that we'll all regret. The thing is, I'm angry as hell that Blade has put me in this position. It should be a choice between one thing or another, not one *person* and another.

He'd made this personal, and it didn't need to be.

Going to the room with the leaves and twigs, I grab a handful, then go to the room with the water. I throw the stuff in it and watch as the fish dart away. Letting my torch light reflect off of the water, I check to make sure nothing sinister is waiting for me, and then I kneel down and use my hand to cup water into my mouth. I do it several times, until I'm sated, and then I use the water to wash my face and my neck.

All the while my thoughts roll through my mind... fight or escape? What was the better choice? If Storm was still down here after all this, we could be fighting for nothing. And if every other group had died, he was right that there was no telling why we would be the ones to escape. But then again, Storm had just yesterday seen that the opening of doorways made openings in the tunnels above us. That seemed to be... grasping at straws. We really didn't know if there was even a chance at escape.

I sense someone behind me. "I haven't decided yet."

Someone slams into me, knocking me to the ground and coming down hard on top of me, and a hand goes over my mouth. I realize it's one of the vampires as I stare into his red, desperate yes. My eyes are wild, and I struggle beneath him.

"Come, brother, drink," he whispers.

His injured brother staggers over and collapses to his knees beside me.

I'm frantic, trying to reach for my powers, even while I know it's nearly impossible when I'm afraid.

The brother leans down and bites my throat on one side, and pain rips through me. I'm shocked at how unlike Blade's bite it is. There's nothing sexual or pleasurable about it, but my terror gives way to a strange numbness. And then the other brother leans over and bites my throat on the other side. Both vampires are groaning and thrashing as they drink and drink, pinning me to the ground.

But I can't fight. I can't do anything.

I don't know how much time passes when they finally draw back, but the hand is still pressed over my mouth. I can feel hot blood flowing over my neck and chest. And both men's mouths are covered in scarlet, but my body still feels numb. Like it doesn't belong to me.

"That's enough," the one on top of me says. "If we kill her, we don't know what will happen."

He lifts his hand from my mouth, and I want to scream, but can't. Both men look at me, and I'm not sure if it's regret or hunger that fills their eyes, but they turn and head back out the door.

The torch lies on the stone, making the shadows dance around me. One of my arms and part of my body lies in the water, and I feel weak and confused. There's a part of me that knows that if I can't get out of the water soon the fish will return, and I'll be torn to pieces. There's another part of me that wonders how much blood one of my kind can lose before they die, but all my thoughts are far away.

Eventually, the torch goes out.

I'm left in darkness, and I feel something in the water bump my hand.

My blood runs cold, and I pray my guys find me before it's too late.

22

STORM

I finally stand. We've been arguing for what feels like hours. The tension in the room is so thick that I truly think we'll come to blows if I stay much longer. In my heart, I know that trying to escape is the best step, but I also know that I'll go where they go now. And that fact angers me above all else, because it seems as if each day that passes my own survival becomes less and less important. Which scares me.

Turning, I head for the door.

"Where are you going?" Blade shouts. "We need to figure this out as men."

I keep walking. "This is not the way men solve problems."

"You mean shifters, right?" He throws back at me. "Shifters don't just talk out problems."

I hesitate in the doorway and look back at him. "Most half-breed shifters are barely sane. You are sane. You are normal. The hate that surrounds you comes from yourself. You hate what you are, not me."

His expression is stunned as I turn back and head down the

hallway. I intend to hide in my space above the demon's tunnels and clear my head. After so long of surviving alone, maybe I simply needed time away from Elizabeth and her men.

But as I walk, I hear the smallest whimper in the darkness. My senses sharpen, and I breathe in deeply, channeling my wolf. Every hair on my body stands on end as I catch the scent of fresh blood. I shift into my wolf form so that the darkness around me is brightened and the scent intensified. Then, I breathe in deeply and follow the smell. It leads me to the room with the water, and I swear my heart stops. I can make out Elizabeth's form, half in the water, and she's covered in something I suspect is blood.

I race to her and nose her body. Her hands lift weakly and wrap around my body.

Hold onto me, I say into her mind.

But when I try to pull her away from the water, she doesn't have the strength to hold me. So I shift back into my human form, and the world becomes darker. I hear the sound of splashing and react without thinking, tossing her over my shoulder as she moans.

I don't slow as I dart from the hall. I just keep running until I leap out into the light of the room with the fire. The three men are on their feet in an instant, first with looks of raw anger, and then with shock. I rush to the blankets and lay her down. If the fish had fed on her... but it isn't fish.

"The vampires," I say, my voice barely louder than a hiss.

The men are around me in an instant. I can scent their fear in the air, and it adds to my own.

"Will she be okay?" Ax asks, and he sounds terrified.

I ignore him. "Bring me the moss in the room with the roots. Only the moss. It's dark green and usually grows around the base of the room."

Gabriel is gone without a word.

I begin to tear one of the blankets with my bare hands.

"We need some water, but be careful of the fish."

This time, Ax is the one to go.

"Is she going to be okay?" Blade asks, his voice betraying his emotion.

When I strain my ears, I can hear her pulse. And it's weak. I have no idea how a half-wraith heals, but from the look of the messy bites at her throat, this had been a lot for her body.

"They tore into her like meat!" He finally says, rising, he slams his hand into the wall.

I'm not usually one to give way to my anger, but I wish I could slam the wall too. I wish I could tear the vampires to pieces and leave them screaming for mercy. And the desire is so damned foreign to me that I freeze for a moment, before continuing to shred the cloth.

The men are back a minute later. I use the water to clean the wounds, and wince as I uncover them. Those vampire bastards were more than capable of leaving clean bites that could heal easily, but they hadn't done so. What was more, she had lost a lot of blood.

Too much blood.

When I'm done cleaning her wounds, I pack the moss onto them. I'd used the moss on my own wounds before. It would help clean them and prevent infection. Then, I wrapped her throat.

It was all I could do for her wounds. Carefully, I clean her body of blood, undress her, and put her in new clothes, all while the men watch. There are moments when I think they'll stop me, but they never do. And I'm glad. Something inside of me wants to wash every last drop of the attack from her body, as if by doing so it'll erase the memory of what happened to her.

It was illogical and told me more than anything else that sleeping with her had been a mistake. Now she was more than just a woman I found attractive. She was more than just a woman who intrigued me, or a woman whose destiny seemed to be tied to my own.

But then, maybe I was in denial. Even before the sex. Even before I saw her. She was *something* to me.

When I'm done, I stand. "All you can do now is watch her. And hope."

I turn and head for the door.

"Where are you going?" Gabriel demands.

I freeze. "I'm going to kill the vampires," the words came out low and dangerous.

"We'll come too," Ax says.

I look back and shake my head. "She's vulnerable and needs to be protected."

Blade rises. "Then they'll stay with her and I'll go with you."

My gaze locks with his. "Are you sure?"

He nods.

We don't take a torch with us, and I hope his vision is as decent in the darkness as mine is, even in human form. "Can you shift?" I ask.

His answer comes slowly. "No."

I nod and decide to remain in my human form too. "That is unusual, but you're not the first shifter I've met who was trapped in their human form."

We move through the dark tunnels, but I can sense him tense beside me. "Really?"

"There was a boy in another family we would trade with. He couldn't shift."

"I've never heard of that before," his words are filled with awe.

"You don't need to shift to be one of us. You don't need to be a full-blood to be part of a pack."

He says nothing.

"I think I'm beginning to see all of you as my pack," I confess. "I just don't want to fail you the way I failed my family."

"How did you fail them?" he asks really slowly.

"I wasn't there to protect them when they needed me," I say.

"I watched my family be murdered as a child and hid. I *hid* and did nothing to help them." His words are barely louder than a whisper.

My mind creates an image of this man as a small boy watching his family die. "So, we both lost people we loved. We both take the blame for their deaths." I release a slow breath. "I hope we can find a way to let this go. Elizabeth deserves men who can forgive themselves. Guilt has a way of destroying good men."

His air rushes out. "I thought you'd be disgusted with me for hiding."

It's strange how much I wish I could hug him. He seems... so young when he's vulnerable. "If you hadn't hidden, you'd be dead too. And your parents' sacrifice would've been for nothing. By living, you defied their enemies, and you did what they wanted you to do. What more honorable thing is there than that?"

He says nothing more as we come to the room with the one lone bulb.

The shifter freezes beside me, and I stop too.

He opens his mouth, then closes it.

I nod, knowing that his heart has words he isn't ready to speak. "Let's kill the vampires."

He looks relieved, and then we take the tunnel to the vampire's home.

I would've loved to shift and tear the vampires apart, but I felt that this would be the wrong thing for my blossoming relationship with Blade, so I don't. Instead, we catch them by surprise and tear the bastards apart, just as we'd promised. They fight, and strengthened by our mate's blood, they're strong, but it's like we're machines hell-bent on revenge. Their claws, their teeth, their weapons, we feel none of it.

And when we're finished, the room is painted in red.

When we come out of the tunnel, the demons are waiting. The leader raises his brow.

We say nothing, just turn and head back to Elizabeth.

His voice calls after us. "Two down, one to go."

He was right. There was just one more group that needed to die. Only, it was his.

23

ELIZABETH

I wake up sure that I'm dead. That this is the next stage in the circle of life. And then the pain hits me and I know I can't be dead.

My eyes crack open, and I see Gabriel and Ax sitting beside me. They both leap up when my eyes open, and then I start to cry. I don't move. It'd hurt too much to move, but I can't stop the tears from rolling down my face.

"Are you okay?" Ax asks, his face going a few shades paler.

Gabriel touches my face, wiping the tears away.

"H-hurts," I whisper.

Gabriel's face goes dark, and I can't tell what he's thinking. Only, he looks like he wants to destroy someone or something.

I keep crying, and he keeps wiping the tears away. Ax gently presses kisses to the top of my head, but none of it helps. The pain in my neck is like nothing I've felt before. I can practically feel my blood pumping in my throat. The nerve-endings screaming from just the work it took to keep me alive.

I hear Storm say, "it's done."

But I can't see him.

Ax pulls back and then Gabriel's gaze locks with mine. "I think I can help," he says, but I have no idea how he can.

He stands, then leans down and picks me up, carrying me gently in his arms. But the movement causes a sharp pain to radiate through my neck, and a hoarse scream tears from my lips.

"What are you doing?" Blade asks.

Gabriel doesn't answer, but he carries me out of the room and into the darkness. A torch follows behind us, and I can feel the other men at our sides. My eyes close, and my head rests on his chest. I have no idea how much time passes when Gabriel says my name.

I bite down on another scream as he lies me down on the ground, but my head lolls painfully to one side. Around me is a room covered in blood, bits of flesh, and severed body parts. I have no idea what I'm looking at until the two wispy spirits rise into the air and dive straight into me.

For a minute my mouth hangs open, and then the strength of the two supernaturals slams into me. Every hair on my body stands on end. My nipples harden. And the pain in my throat fades away.

"Better?" Gabriel asks, his voice rough.

"Yes," my voice still comes out harsh.

He picks me up again, and this time I don't scream. They take me back to our safe little home and they lie me back on the bed and cover me with blankets. Storm gently looks beneath my bandages, and I wince as new pain awakens.

"How does she look?" Blade asks, but he won't look at me.

"Better. But it's not enough."

Ax's voice comes out low and threatening. "What if this time we kill the demons and make sure they stay dead."

Storm shakes his head. "I can guarantee you that they're expecting it, and that they're probably even planning to take us out."

Gabriel swears.

"So what do we do?" Ax asks. "How much time before the next challenge?"

Storm's quiet for a long minute. "My guess? Tomorrow."

"That's not enough time." Ax looks down at his hands.

No one speaks for a long time until Gabriel does. "I changed my vote. Tomorrow we try to escape. Until then, we try to survive."

Storm gives a sharp nod. "We should eat and clean up, watching our backs every second, and then I have a place we can hide."

Blade is suddenly squeezing my hand. "What do you think, Elizabeth?"

What do I think? I'm not much use right now, even if I can feel the spirits of the two vampires inside of me. Whatever challenge we might face next, I'm not sure I'll survive.

"I think... it's a plan."

Everyone gets to work, but I don't move, I just lay there. This all feels so surreal. Just a short time ago we were all preparing to battle together, but now it seemed they were just trying to make sure I survived. The thought made my stomach hurt.

What if my weakness leads to all our deaths?

24

AX

We all ate and washed up in a hurry, then loaded up with weapons. There was just something in the air. A warning. I could feel the darkness so deep that it seemed to be growing within me to the point where I felt like running or fighting, anything rather than prepping for the unknown. I was more than a little thankful when Storm had taken us to a hiding place above the demon's tunnel to wait and watch.

Unfortunately, we hadn't needed to wait long. I was the first look out, and within an hour or two of coming to our hiding place, the demons had snuck out. Their weapons had been drawn, and they'd moved through the tunnel with deliberate care, heading straight for our tunnel.

Once they were gone, I hadn't woken the others. We needed our rest for the next challenge. But I'd watched as eventually they left our tunnel and went to the vampire's home, and then down the elementalist's tunnel. At that point, I did wake the others, and we all sat there in the darkness, watching for them to come back out and realize that we'd effectively disappeared.

They'd continued to search for hours before finally returning to their tunnel. We'd all breathed a sigh of relief then, and I'd gone to sleep, leaving Storm to keep an eye out. By the time Gabriel had shaken me awake, I didn't have a clue what time it was, but I knew a great deal of time had passed.

"Elizabeth?" I whisper automatically.

"I'm here," she says, her voice so sleepy that I want to wrap my arms around her.

"How are you?"

She hesitates. "A little better..."

But something in her voice tells me she's still struggling, and it's like a knife twisting in my gut. In my mind, I can picture the moment Storm brought her to us. If he hadn't gotten her out of the water in time, I didn't even want to think about what would happen, but I knew she wouldn't still be with us. And whatever Gabriel and Blade thought of him, I owed him everything for saving her life. If not my own life, then at least my loyalty.

"Something's happening," Gabriel whispers.

Tension hangs between us. Everyone begins to shift and stretch, and then I hear it too. The crackling of the speaker. The muscles in my neck are taunt as I wait for the sound of the warden's voice. But, I hear the demons first. The men are muttering as they walk under us to the room with the one lone bulb. When they're further from our spot, I move and lay partially on my belly, so that I can see them in the center of the room. The others move so we can all see some part of them.

The warden's voice came over the speaker, and every hair on my body stood on end. "Go into... the room. First group... reach the other side... wins. Everyone else... dies."

We all held perfectly still as the stone began to shake,

and then Storm launches into action. I can see his outline by the bulb, and we all follow him as part of the stone above us opens. He goes first, followed by Elizabeth, then Gabriel, Blade, and I follow at the end. We all stumble along together, searching for an opening above us. Desperation fills the air, and then after a minute, Storm shouts.

"There's no way out. Run! Back to the door!"

We scramble back the way we'd come, and I almost fall through the hole we'd climbed down. "The hole's right here!" I say, climbing down.

I hear them behind me, so I keep rushing forward, knowing that I have to get to that door. The stone around us begins to shake again. I drop down to the demon's tunnel and race for the door. It's halfway down when I duck under it, and then I begin to shift, growing bigger and bigger and lifting the door. The others came running a second later. Elizabeth looks pale, but otherwise much better, and they duck under the door. I release it as I bend into the room, and then let my size grow smaller.

Then, I'm at the rear of our group again.

Storm's voice came to me from the front of our party. "The demons got a huge head start. We're going to need a miracle to live."

We explode out into a massive room. And when I say massive, I mean massive. It must have occupied most of the space beneath the entire prison. Or at least our part of the prison. In front of us is a red veil of light, and the demons are far ahead in what could only be described as an obstacle course. They're swinging on monkey bars across a pit of spikes. The leader reaches the other side and turns back to us with a grin.

"Fucking hell," Gabriel says. "I can't use my powers."

"The red light probably messes with our powers, so don't count on it."

The fourth demon misses one of the bars. His eyes widen, and then his other hand slips. He plummets onto the stakes, and they pierce his body. Tearing through his chest in multiple places, his shoulders, and even his legs. Blood spurts from his mouth, and his eyes go glassy.

"Do you think they're still coming back to life?" I ask.

Storm starts forward. "It doesn't matter. We need to be faster than them."

We all move through the red light, and it feels strange, like an oil on my skin. When I reach the other side, I reach for my ability to shift, but nothing happens. *Damn it.* Whatever the red light was, it had done something to my powers.

"Elizabeth--" Gabriel starts.

"I got this," she says, then surprises all of us by rushing forward.

Storm overtakes her and darts around pools of bubbling black stuff. She follows quickly behind, and Blade follows her, then Gabriel is in front of me. I think we all want to surround Elizabeth as well as possible, so we're there to help her if she needs it.

"Damn it," I mutter. My attention was so focused on Elizabeth that when one of the black bubbles popped, it splattered partially on my pants. Within seconds, the material had melted and burned my flesh. It wasn't a bad injury, but it was a stupid injury, especially this early in the challenge.

I grit my teeth and will myself to focus on surviving, not the woman I love.

We get through the bubbling pits, then come to a small metal path that weaves through a lake filled with a black substance that looks strangely like the acidic bubbles. I imagine what the popping bubble did to my leg and wince.

If we fall in that... we're done for... in a *very* painful way. And the path through it is barely as wide as a foot, and just inches above the dangerous-looking water.

Shit. My stomach flips, but I keep running toward it.

Storm slows as he reaches the edge of it and takes the path carefully. We all follow suit.

It's not easy. Sweat rolls down my back, and my gaze darts from the metal path to the others ahead of us. Blade wavers at one point, and I'm ready and willing to grab him and keep him steady, but he recovers, and I'm glad he does. Some logical part of me thinks I'm less likely to save him than I am to go down with him.

It takes us less than a couple of minutes to get to the other side, but the demons have disappeared somewhere down a slope in the distance. I can hear them grunting, but nothing else.

Storm reaches the monkey bars over the spikes first, but turns to Elizabeth. "Go first. I'll grab you if you start to slip."

Gabriel opens his mouth to no doubt argue, but she nods, and Storm lifts her up so that she's grabbing the bars. One after another we follow her, and it's not easy. The bars are slick, and it takes considerable effort to keep from slipping. It seems that every time I've grabbed the next bar, my fingers are barely clinging to the last one.

Suddenly, Elizabeth cries out. I look around the guys, and see her fall. My heart catches in my throat, but Storm has her by the back of her shirt. And her feet? They're posed on the demon's body. The spirit of the demon rises up and slams into her, and as much as I'm glad because I know it'll make her stronger, I swear I don't breathe while she teeters over those spikes.

Storm lifts her up, sweat on his brow, and she grabs the bars once more. We keep going, but our rhythm is off, and my heart is racing. We need to reach the other side soon. My arms are aching. My palms are sweaty. And one near-miss was more than enough.

Just keep going. Just keep going.

But remember, not all of you need to make it until the end. Just you. I stiffen at the strange thought, and that sense of something dark uncurling inside of me comes again. I push it aside. It was time to focus, not dwell on that strange feeling.

When my feet hit the other side, Blade pulls me fully away from the pit and to safety.

We all stand for a minute, panting.

"Ready?" Storm says, and I wish I could tell him, *hell no*, but I nod.

We start up the hill made of stone. Dirt slowly begins to cover the stone, and when we come down the other side, we see a patch of trees. Instantly I think of the sentient beings. The trees are made of the same combination of strange twigs and brown and green grass, wrapped all around the trees like something strange and wrong.

I hesitate. "Think it's another trap?"

Elizabeth lifts a brow. "I'm pretty much prepared for everything in this place to beat the crap out of us."

"Fun. Okay." I force a smile, and wink at her.

A strange look comes over her face, like she's relieved, which doesn't make any sense. But then she turns around, and we keep going. Some unsettling feeling follows me as we go.

On the other side of the trees is a river of some kind with no way to cross. It's a wide river. And on the other side, one of the demons is climbing out. He's covered in blood, and pulls one of the scary flesh eater fish off of his leg, tossing it back into the water. His leg is missing a massive chunk of flesh, and my stomach turns at the thought of Elizabeth swimming in the water.

"The trees," Storm says.

And it hits me.

We all go and start pulling the leaves and twigs off of the trees until our arms are full, and then we stand along the edge, staring down at the water filled with the monstrous creatures. Behind us, we make certain the trees aren't going to suddenly launch into an attack, then release a slow breath when nothing bad happens and look back at the water.

"Drop them," Storm says, and we do.

The instant the twigs and leaves hit the water, the fish dart away, far out of sight.

"Will it keep them away in a body of water this big?" Blade asks, not sounding convinced.

"Maybe on this side. I'm not sure about the other," Storm says, "so tread lightly."

We enter the water as a group. Elizabeth swimming in the center of us. I keep a dagger in one hand, and try to search for any signs of the creatures in the water ahead of me while swimming as fast as humanly possible. Storm seems confident as he moves, but when we're nearly to the other side of the shore, he cries out. I see a flash of silver in front of me and stab out without thinking. The massive fish on my blade makes a horrible sound, and I pull it free and throw it, then keep going.

I hear Gabriel grunt, and Blade swear, and then we're on the other side. Storm hauls Elizabeth out of the water almost faster than I can follow, and then we all struggle out. Blade and Gabriel are bleeding. Blade from his shoulder, and Gabriel from his stomach, but they look angry rather than hurt.

"Are you okay?" Gabriel asks Elizabeth.

She looks annoyed. "You guys are the ones bleeding... and don't think I haven't noticed you keep trying to be a wall of bodies around me. Not that I don't appreciate it."

"Absorbing souls makes you strong," Gabriel says, his gaze intense as it lands on the bandages around her neck. "But you're still healing."

She rolls her eyes. "I remember."

He actually laughs and shakes his head. Which is kind of awesome. Gabriel isn't exactly the kind of guy who smiles easily. And somehow, that makes me love Elizabeth even more.

"So, keep going? she asks, quirking her brow.

"You bet," Blade says. "We need to beat those fucking demons."

"And kill them. Remember, they can die here." She grins.

Somehow her bloodthirst seems to bring us all strength. That was one thing about our Elizabeth. She had every reason in the world to just lay down and be scared, or fall into her pain, but she never did. We'd all had hard lives, and this was difficult for us. I didn't know what kept her going.

Storm gestures for us to continue, and we do, but my gaze lingers on the beautiful red-head for a long moment before I refocus. Up ahead is a black wall of light that separates us from what looks to be a wide empty space. Again, we can't see the demons.

"This place isn't what it seems," Elizabeth says softly. "I think we all saw that big obstacle course, but it's different as we're going through it, like it's changing. What we saw might've been some kind of illusion."

Storm's brows rise. "I think you're right. It seems each new challenge isn't something I saw when we first came to the room. And this room looks innocent, but nothing is innocent here."

Again, we move to flank Elizabeth. This time Blade is at her back. We move through the black light and that oily feeling on my skin returns. But even on the other side of the light, the space seems entirely empty. Except, impossibly so, everything we've already faced seems to be gone behind us. There are simply stone walls on both sides of us, and the black light concealing everything beyond that. Torches light the walls, and then there's a small, dark doorway up ahead.

"Can anyone use their magic?" Blade asks softly.

There's a chorus of *nos*. We creep forward through the room, but nothing stirs. I'm starting to feel more and more nervous when we hit the center of the room, and then all hell breaks loose. Swinging blades on chains explode from the walls, raining chunks of stone onto the ground and raising a cloud of dust into the air. They come at us from every direction, and I don't even think when I grab Elizabeth, throw her over my shoulder, and jump onto the top of one of the blades, holding the chain to keep from falling.

Luckily, the others make the same split-second decision. We're swinging from the chains, our feet resting on the flat top of the blades. We swing back and forth and back and forth, safe, but having no clue how to get out of there. The tips of the blades almost skim the ground, and lift up higher as they reach the edges of the room, but not high enough for us to duck down under and escape death.

For a second, we all seem to be frozen. And I'm sure they're doing the same thing I am, studying the blades to see any weaknesses in the room. Any path we could take through them and not end up dead.

Unfortunately, I see nothing. No escape. No way to survive this.

That's because death clings to this place, waiting to claim one of the people you love. The words seem to hiss through my mind, so real that I stiffen and glance around, even though I know they were only in my mind.

What the hell is happening to me?

"We need to jump from one to the next one to reach the door," Gabriel says, then his gaze meets mine. "Do you have her?"

My mind snaps back to our current situation, and my gaze tracks the swinging blades again. He's right, we do need to jump across the blades. That's the only way. But the truth is, as strong as I am, I don't think I can leap from one blade to the next with her on me.

"Put me down. I can do this," she says over my shoulder.

Gabriel frowns, his gaze darting from her to the blades.

I want to keep her safe, but I trust her ability to do this on her own more than I trust mine to be fast enough and light enough to make these jumps quickly, so I slowly slide her down my body until her hands grip the chain, and we're standing pressed against each other.

Her eyes meet mine. "I got this," she reassures me.

I can't help it, I kiss her lips lightly. "You better."

She shifts to face the next blade, and I watch as Storm suddenly leaps from one, to the next, to the next, and finally lands in the doorway, before darting in. He watches us from the shadows, his expression blank. Blade follows his path, moving slower, calculating each jump before he does it, and then Storm moves out of the way when he jumps in the doorway.

Gabriel jumps to the next blade, then looks back, waiting for Elizabeth. I know it's crazy that we want to stay close to her when I doubt we could save her in time if we slip, but we do. Our progress across the swinging blades is almost painfully slow, and then we reach the doorway and dart inside. In the shadows of that hall, we all take a moment, and my racing heart slows, if only by a fraction.

"There's definitely something weird about this place," Elizabeth says.

Suddenly, we hear a roar down the hall that seems to shake the very stone. We all turn at once and look into the darkness. Whatever was there, I had no doubt it was our next challenge.

I just hoped it was something we could survive.

25

ELIZABETH

I was so fucking angry. Or maybe it wasn't anger. Maybe it was that those vampire spirits, along with the demon spirit, were swelling inside of me, begging to be used. Or released. Images of the wisps inside of me bursting out, tearing my enemies to shreds at Nightmare Penitentiary flash through my mind. Now that I knew everything my magic could do, and had the wisps inside of me, I prayed I'd be less of a liability to my men, and more of a strength.

The roar sounds again, and we keep inching through the hallway toward the bright room on the other side. I try to think back to what this area had looked like when we all stood in the doorway earlier, but I can't quite recall. All I have is a vague sense of a room with a huge obstacle course.

That alone is enough to make me believe that magic is involved.

We stop when we come to the end of the hall. Before us is a massive room. And in the center, an ogre, easily a story tall is in the center of the room... eating one of the demons. Half the demon's body is still held in the ogre's hand, blood gushing from it, and he's chewing on the top half of the demon. For a second an arm hangs out of his mouth, and then he slurps it up.

"I'm going to be sick," Ax whispers.

My own stomach turns.

On the other side of the room, the two remaining demons scramble for cover in a doorway. If I didn't know better, I'd think their plan was to sacrifice the man so they could escape.

"We need to go now, while it's feeding," Storm says.

Gabriel draws himself up taller. "We all run for the other side of the door. Elizabeth in the front. If he comes for us, we split off and distract him."

"What?" I turn. "No."

He shoves me forward, and then we're all running, and I don't have any choice but to keep going. And even though I'm terrified out of my mind, I promise myself Gabriel will get the talking to of his life for his stunt, and this stupid plan.

When I'm not running for my life.

My heartbeat fills my ears and my feet pound against the stone. We're halfway across when the ogre tosses the rest of the demon in the air and starts to bite down on him. Blood splurts, trailing down his chin, and I hear the haunting sound of bones crushing. Bile rises in the back of my throat, but I focus on the door.

And then, he roars again and every hair on my body stands on end.

I chance a look back at him, and he's looking right at us. He starts forward, his step shaking the entire room. We're almost there. *Just a little further.* I just pray my men stay focused on the door and don't foolishly change directions as Gabriel said. If they get caught in the room, they're doomed.

Another step shakes the earth, and then another.

"Keep going!" I cry, panting.

And then the ogre roars again. His steps change direction, and I look behind me and see that sure enough all three of my men are going in different directions. The ogre is heading for Blade, and the idiot is going for the corner. *What the hell does he think will happen once he gets there?*

I skid to a halt. "The door! It's the only way!"

None of them listen to me. I feel my powers swirling around inside of me, and reach for them. It feels as if there's a sticky veil between me and my powers, but I grit my teeth and keep pushing. Something in me knows this is magic programmed to stop us. But my powers? No one has seen them before, as far as I know, so maybe the veil won't work against me.

The ogre is still heading for Blade when my mate reaches the corner. He turns and pulls out his sword, ready and willing to fight. But a sword will do nothing against a beast this size, and we all know it.

Gabriel, Storm, and Ax are suddenly running at me again. Gabriel waves for me to run through the door, and I know deep in their hearts that they don't expect Blade to survive this. Which pisses me off.

We're all going to make it out.

I won't lose any of them, I swear it.

Closing my eyes, I lift my hands and focus on the swirling wisps of souls inside of me. The veil continues to separate us, but I just keep pushing and pushing until I feel it snap. The ogre is reaching for Blade. Blade stabs it with his sword, and the ogre laughs, grabbing Blade and lifting him into the air.

I curse and grab all the souls, focus on the ogre, and push my powers out like a force of nature. The ogre explodes, blood, guts, and God-only-knew what else covers me. I reach up and smear the disgusting mess off my face and open my eyes. The entire room looks like a massacre. A pile of flesh moves, and Blade suddenly stands out of it.

"Fuck, that's gross!" he shouts.

My heart squeezes. "But you're alive right?"

Gabriel is in front of me in an instant. "You can use your magic?"

I feel inside myself. It's still there, but I've spent a lot of it.

I nod.

"Mine's still not working. Anyone else?"

There's a chorus of *nos*.

He wipes more blood out of his hair and smiles. "Well, that's something."

Blade jogs back over to us. We're all a mess. But I don't care, because we're all alive. I pull Blade into a quick, disgusting, hug, trying not to think about the moment the ogre picked him up. Then release him, and we both smile before looking at the others.

"It's nice that we survived this far, but none of this matters," Storm finally says. "If they beat us to the end, we're dead."

"That's cheery," I mutter.

"He's right. We need to keep going." Ax's has that strange look on his face again. The one that I can't quite place, but it's gone in a flash.

He smiles at me. I try to ignore the flutter in my stomach.

We all head to the other doorway and run through the dark tunnel. There's light on the other side, just like the lighted room with the ogre. This time no one says it, but we all pull out our swords and approach cautiously. As we inch out, the light's blinding for a painful second.

And then it comes into focus. To one side of the room is what looks like a massive mountain, climbing up into the darkness far above us. Two torches burn by a plaque at the bottom of the mountain. Two more torches burn alongside the wall directly across from us. There's a door lighted with bulbs. Golden. Etched with a language I don't understand. And then there's another door to one corner. It's wooden. Simple. And something about it calls to me.

But I also realize that the giant mountain beneath the prison, and the wall with lighted doors, can't logically exist in this space. It's like I'm looking into another world when I look toward the mountain, and like my vision shifts when I turn to the wall.

Whatever magic they used for this obstacle course was like nothing I've ever imagined.

My gaze snaps back to the wooden door. It's hard to take my eyes off of it for a long minute when I see the air change around it. Suddenly, my father, the wraith himself, is standing by the door. I can feel within him a strange kind of panic, and I know that appearing for me costs him and that he can't remain here for long.

He taps the wooden door. "Choose it." Then vanishes.

My heart races, and I look at my guys. None of them seem to have seen him. They start forward toward the plaque, and we all stop in front of it. The plaque reads, "get the key from the top of the mountain and get your freedom. Choose correctly."

We exchange a glance, then look back at the mountain.

"I guess we're climbing it?" I say.

Ax sighs. "At least this seems to be the last challenge. Hopefully."

"The last challenge is usually the one everyone dies on," Storm says softly.

This guy can be so positive sometimes...

"Not this time," I tell him, willing myself to sound confident, then step forward.

The air shimmers around me as I walk toward the mountain, and within seconds, everything changes. It's like I've stepped into a new world. The air is cold and carries with it the scents of fall, which is shockingly pleasant after my time in the prison. There are thick, towering trees around me, and a forest stretching out in all directions. I even see a crescent moon in the sky just overhead.

And yet, that initial elation at being somewhere other than a dark prison fades away, and I shiver. Something about this place is so much worse than the prison, like the monsters that haunt these shadows are just better at hiding. The feeling intensifies with each moment that passes, and a chill rolls up my spine. I'm left staring between the trees, heart pounding, waiting for something terrible.

Then, it hits me.

What the hell is this place to create such intense fear inside of me?

I'm not sure what to think about this last challenge, except I sense death.

My guys come to stand at my side, and I breathe in a ragged breath, overwhelmed by the heaviness of the pain and suffering in the air.

Death is all around us. This isn't good.

26

BLADE

This is a kind of magic I've never seen before. The mountain is thick with fog as we move deeper in the woods, and I can sense the creatures that hide in the shadows. My fangs elongate, and I have a moment of relief that at least our powers seem to have been returned to us. I inch forward, determination pulsing through me. No doubt the demons were somewhere ahead of us. There was no way I would let them win, and allow Elizabeth to die in this dark place. I didn't care what I had to do to keep her safe, but I would.

"This place is dangerous," Storm says behind me.

"At least we have our powers," I tell him.

Gabriel's voice is strong and angry. "Is this what the challenges are usually like?"

Storm hesitates, then speaks. "No, something is off about this one and this place. They don't usually waste this much magic on the challenges."

"Great," Ax says dryly.

"So what's the plan?" I ask.

As much as I hated looking to Storm for guidance, I did.

He was the one with the most experience in here, and that counted for a hell of a lot right now.

"We use our powers. We stick together, and we get the key. Then, we see if this actually ends in our freedom."

I'm starting to really like this Storm. "Agreed."

Gabriel leads us. And I'm glad he does. I can practically feel his dark powers swirling around him. Any creature foolish enough to step in his way is going to pay. Storm shifts into his massive white wolf form, and I clench the sword in my hands tighter. Elizabeth stands in the middle of us, her own sword in her hand.

We creep forward and barely make it a few steps into the fog when some kind of mutated beast covered in gray fur leaps out at us. It's head snaps to one side, and then it falls in a crumpled mass in front of us. When I look at Gabriel, his eyes are filled with fury.

Continuing forward, I can sense the creatures, but none come forward for a while. We start up a worn path on the base of the mountain, and something darts at us out of the sky. The thing bursts like a pinata, raining feathers and flesh on us.

"Elizabeth," Ax groans.

"You're alive, aren't you?" she says, a slight smile in her voice.

We keep going, dusting feathers and flesh off of us as we go, and then a few small rocks tumble from above onto the path. We all freeze, exchange a look, then keep going. Something was sure as hell above us, something not good, but the only choice we had was to face it when we had to.

We wind around and around the mountain, and the air grows colder, and the fog thicker. I can just barely make out the peaks of the trees sticking out of the fog, and motion in the sky, but nothing more.

Not being able to see much was unsettling. Worse than even the darkness in the tunnels, although I wasn't sure why.

The path grew smaller and smaller until we had to put away our swords and use our hands to grip onto the side of the mountain in order to continue climbing on the path. Well, everyone except Storm, his wolf was agile as it climbed around the mountain, even on the narrow path.

And then, more small rocks tumble down onto us from above.

I stop and squint up. There was something hidden in the fog. *Something dangerous.* Using my shifter abilities, I scent the air, tasting the fog and nature, blood, and something I could never remember scenting before. My fangs seem to ache in my mouth, so for once both my shifter side and my vampire side were in agreement.

Unfortunately, they're in agreement that some unknown monster is waiting for us in the mountains above us.

I'm about to warn the others when a sharpened talon reaches down and grabs me by the shoulder. A cry escapes my lips as the creature drags me off of the path and into the fog. Its talon digs into my shoulder, and I strike out over and over again with my fist, putting my supernatural strength into each blow. A screech explodes from whatever the hell it is, and then I'm falling. My hands scramble for purchase on the side of the mountain, but I can't seem to stop my descent when a hand catches me.

For a second, I'm dangling in mid-air, and then Ax says, "for the love of god, get your footing, you heavy asshole."

I try to climb up, and one of my feet hits a ledge. I push up on it and get my other foot next to me, then the hand that grabs my shirt pushes me against the side of the mountain. Panting, I turn and see Ax grinning beside me, but there's fear behind his eyes.

"What the fuck was that?"

I shake my head. "I don't know, but it's not good."

We keep going, but I hear Storm's low growl of warning. We make it around the mountain once more when suddenly Storm begins to growl again. Everyone stops, and I pull out my sword, then press the sword and my hand back on the mountain. Sure enough, that damn talon darts out, and I cut it off with one smooth movement. A screech tears through the fog, and I hear the sounds of my friends fighting beside me. One talon wraps around Elizabeth and starts to drag her up, but Storm leaps at it and chomps down on something above us. There's another terrible screech that gets louder and shriller, and he drops, just barely managing to get purchase on the ledge.

Gabriel makes a motion with one hand, and a dark creature falls above him and plummets down. It's a long minute before we hear it hit the ground far below.

"Rock... spiders," Ax says beside me, breathless, and swinging his own sword above him.

"Rock spiders?" I repeat in disbelief.

"They're big, mean, and hungry," he pants. "And usually, when you find one of them, you find the nest."

We keep going and round a corner. Thankfully, the path widens and then we find ourselves on a plateau of some kind. The fog swirls around us, and rocks crunch beneath our feet. It feels as if we're walking above the clouds in a fantasy world of magic and mystery.

Except we're not superheroes and the best thing we can hope for is to survive all of this.

Everything is eerily silent around us as we continue crunching forward, our steps slow and careful. The wind whips around us, and Elizabeth looks back at me, and her red-hair moves in the breeze behind her. For a second, I'm transfixed by her. How was I lucky enough to find a woman who was both beautiful and brave?

I force a smile that I'm sure isn't reassuring at all, but she gives a small smile in return, and then refocuses on whatever might be ahead of us. And then a cave appears out of the fog like a pirate ship sailing through clouds.

"I'm not going in there," Ax whispers.

I couldn't agree more.

Gabriel leads us around it, and we start up a wider path that runs above the cave.

But we don't make it ten steps before dark shapes begin to emerge from the cave beneath us. I hear them striking the path, and then dozens of dog-sized spiders are suddenly racing at us. The first one crumples over and dies, thanks to Gabriel. The second one bursts, thanks to my beautiful mate. The third one is nearly on me when I strike it with my sword, over and over again. Storm growls behind me and leaps onto the next one, his teeth tearing into the spider while it lets out the worst whining sounds I've ever heard.

More spiders fall over dead. More burst.

But they keep coming.

"I think we need to outrun them," I pant stabbing one and then another.

There's a break in the spiders as they try to climb over their dead brethren.

Gabriel shouts, "keep going!" behind me, and then we all start running.

Every time I look back, the dark shapes are still chasing us through the fog. We round the mountain once, then again, then break out onto another plateau. As we rush forward, and look back, the spiders all stop, then turn around and head back the way they came. One after another the shapes vanish into the fog, and we're all left out-of-breath and confused.

"What the hell?" Ax says.

I frown, staring at where the spiders should be still barreling toward us. "Why did they stop?"

"I can't imagine it's for a good reason," Elizabeth says.

My thoughts exactly.

We turn back to this new part of the mountain. I swear, if I squint above us, I can make out the very top of the mountain not far from us. Suddenly, the dark top of the mountain seems to detach, and before I can shout in warning, something slams through my chest.

Mind-numbing pain cracks through my body, and I open my mouth to scream, but only blood comes out. Instinctually, I try to struggle, only to discover I'm pinned to a rock. My sword falls from my hand, and my arms drop uselessly to my side. An overwhelming sense of uselessness hovers at the back of my mind, but my pure agony makes it impossible to think clearly.

"Blade!" Elizabeth yells my name, but the sounds seems far away.

Whatever pins me through the chest shifts, and this time I hear myself screaming as the massive thing in my chest moves, awakening new stabbing pains that have me wishing for death. A second later, a creature looms above me. It's horrifying. A monster. A half-woman, half-spider. Her face is pale with deep black eyes and her lips are the color of blood. Her torso connects with the spider-half, and she grins down at me.

Elizabeth leaps forward and starts to hack at the leg that pins me down.

Another leg strikes out at her, but Ax knocks her out of

the way just in time. I see them fall together, and then Elizabeth is pointing a hand at the spider, but the creature doesn't explode. Gabriel's pointing at it too, but the spider doesn't fall over dead.

Storm growls and races around, disappearing from view.

And then the spider woman leans down over me. Her mouth opens, and I stare into the terrifying mouth of the beast. Goop spits from her mouth, and I'm suddenly being wrapped. I try to struggle, to fight, but I've lost all control of my body.

I hear Elizabeth and Ax yelling. I know they're fighting for me, even though I can't see them anymore. And yet, I have no idea how they're going to save me from this. Even in my heart, I had an overwhelming sense of hopelessness.

This is it. I'm going to die being eaten alive by a giant spider creature.

27

ELIZABETH

My powers aren't working on the monster. Gabriel's aren't either. I hack at its legs, but it doesn't seem to notice. Gabriel is stabbing his sword into its belly. But it has some kind of hard outer-shell, like a crab, and our blows can't seem to crack its surface. I can only see Blade's face now, and his expression is lax, which is even more terrifying than if he looked scared.

I think of how spiders kill, and my stomach turns. I *have* to stop her. I *have* to save Blade.

Desperate, I rush away from her leg and try to step between her and Blade. The creature's face is horrifying. Partially human, partially covered in the black shell like the rest of her spider body. I stab at its face, and it jerks back and hisses. Another talon comes at me, and I dart and roll to avoid it. But I barely have time to stand when it's stabbing at me again.

I try over and over to use my powers on it, to no success.

The sharp talon slides through the back of my shirt, and I have to rip the material in order to escape. The spider monster hisses at me again, then turns back to Blade. A black straw stretches out from its open mouth and it leans over him.

Storm is suddenly on her back. The massive dog bites into the side of her human-like neck and tears. She shrieks, a terrible sound that seems to shake the very mountain. Her legs try to jab at Storm, but she can't seem to reach him. The leg pinning Blade to the rock pulls back, releasing him so that he crumples to the ground, leaving behind a rock streaked with blood, and I rush forward. Gabriel is suddenly at my side, and we drag him behind the rock.

I touch his face, but he doesn't respond. My heart squeezes, and I feel like I've been punched in the chest. *My sweet Blade...*

"I got it," Gabriel huffs and starts to use his sword to cut away the spider's web.

My legs tremble. There's nothing else I can do for him until he's free of the web. The spider monster shrieks again, and the ground continues to shake.

I rise and watch as the creature tries over and over again, swaying on the mountain, becoming more and more frantic, to reach Storm. Her legs slip over the edge of the mountain, and my mouth opens in a scream as she goes tumbling off the edge. My gaze finds the massive white wolf on her back, and then he disappears from view over the edge. I race after him, then stop at the edge, looking down.

There's nothing but fog. Nothing at all. And then, the world shakes as the monster no doubt hits the ground.

I collapse to my knees, numb. "Storm! Storm!"

My gaze searches the fog. The man had survived every challenge. Dozens and dozens of them. He was strong, and capable, that beast couldn't possibly be the end of him. *Could it?*

I start to cry, my heart in my throat, my gaze skidding

over everything below us. All the moments I've spent with Storm since coming here flash through my mind, and a hollowness grows inside of me until I feel like I can't pull in enough air.

Ax is suddenly at my side. Slowly, he kneels down beside me, and he squeezes my shoulder before saying, "I'm sorry," and there's a finality to his words that somehow make this moment even worse.

"No." A sob explodes from my lips. "He has to be okay... maybe it broke his fall."

"Maybe," he says, but he sounds doubtful.

I hear movement behind me, and turn. Blade is leaning against Gabriel. Gabriel's shirt is gone, but the dark material has been torn and circles the wound in Blade's belly.

"Is he...?" Blade asks, and I know he could only be talking about Storm.

"Yeah," Ax says, the word surprisingly cold.

"He could have made it," I tell them, my voice pleading.

Storm might not have gone through Nightmare Penitentiary with the guys. He might not have fought at our side when we first escaped, but he was a part of our group now. He was one of us. We couldn't just let him die. Not after everything he'd done for us.

Not after everything he meant to me.

And then, it hits me. Something inside of me feels a loss like nothing imaginable. It shocks me. I've lost people I cared for before, but it didn't feel like this. Like part of my heart had been torn out.

"I-- I think I loved him."

All the guys are quiet for a minute.

"He was a nice guy," Ax says.

"He knew how to fight," Gabriel adds.

After a second, Blade softly says, "he was growing on me."

I stand, gripping my sword. "We need to go down and look for him. If he's hurt, if he needs us--"

"He won't have survived that fall," Gabriel says, regret in his voice.

"And even if he did," Ax speaks really slowly, "which is doubtful, none of us will live if the demons get the key first."

"We can't just abandon him!" I shout at them.

When none of them move, I start back to the path going down.

Gabriel grabs my arm. "He's gone, Elizabeth."

I jerk my arm from his. "Would you want me to give up on you so easily?"

His eyes widen.

"Storm was important to me!" I shout.

And then, we hear him. "Glad... to... hear... it."

My eyes widen, and we all watch as a hand appears at the top of the cliff. Ax and Blade are there in an instant, hauling him back over the edge. He's naked, filthy, and bleeding, but he's alive. I run to him and wrap my arms around him in a tight hug.

He says, "*oof*," as I crash into him, but then his arms go around me.

"I thought I lost you," I say, blinking back tears. "I wanted to go get you."

"Thanks for not letting her," he says over my head, and he sounds genuine.

I pull back from him and cup his cheeks. "You're *thanking* them for telling me not to help you?"

"I'm thanking them for keeping my mate alive."

I hear the intake of surprised breaths behind me.

I stare into those pale eyes of him. "I'm your mate?"

He nods and leans forward and kisses me. "I knew so much. I thought I knew everything. This connection between us confused me, but I didn't know what it was to have a mate. When I was falling, a part of me said that this was the end, and then I thought of you, and... I fought. I scrambled for purchase and caught the edge of the mountain. I pulled myself up, and every second I thought of you, and nothing but you. It was like my head and brain were finally talking, and there was no denying what you are to me."

"You're sure?" I ask in disbelief.

He kisses me again. "Yes. I saw you die so many times. I thought you were just special because of my visions. I didn't realize that you were my mate, until now."

Suddenly, Storm looks behind me. "Can you guys handle that?"

They're quiet for a long minute.

Then Blade says, "if we survive, then we'll deal with it."

To my surprise, Storm smiles. "Deal."

I help Storm stand and then we all look to the last part of the mountain.

"If the keys are there, we've won," Storm says.

"And if they're not?" I ask.

Storm squeezes my waist. "Then at least we die together."

We shuffle up the last of the mountain. Elizabeth helps Storm, although I think he doesn't need it. I think they mostly want to keep holding each other, which surprisingly doesn't bother me. *How many times can the guy step between us and death before I have to come to terms with him?*

Apparently, the last time was enough.

There's still so much we have to learn about him, but I trust him. Maybe in the past he survived these challenges, and the teams he worked with died, but this time, he'd admitted Elizabeth was his mate. Even the coldest bastard of a shifter couldn't let his mate die, and that meant I doubly trusted him.

Our pathetic group makes it to the top where *two* keys sit on platforms. A wooden one and a golden one. I don't hesitate, I grab both of them, and then stare down at them. This meant... we'd won? I couldn't believe it. We reached the keys first. And maybe after this twisted challenge we'd just end up in another fucking prison, but at least this didn't mean instant death.

"So... two doors and two keys," I say.

"It's the wooden one."

We all look at Elizabeth.

"How can you be so sure?"

Her gaze meets mine. "Trust me. We use the wooden key on the wooden door, and we win."

"The golden one makes more sense," Ax says. "I mean, why make a shining golden door if it's not the right one?"

She shakes her head. "Just go with me on this."

Storm adds slowly, "I agree with Ax. These men like the show. I have no doubt that they observe every challenge. Somehow. The wooden door is likely the end for the losers."

The wooden door or the golden door? Which one should we choose? I had no idea.

I sigh. "Let's get down, then we'll figure it out."

Ax circles the edge of the top of the mountain. "Uh, guys, I think I found a quick way down."

We all head over and then stare down at a slide of sorts carved into the side of the mountain.

"No fucking way."

Elizabeth laughs. "You're more scared of the slide than the man-eating spiders?"

She has a point.

"This is often the way of the games," Storm adds. "The slide was meant to be used."

"Fuck," I say again.

As a kid I wasn't exactly the type to go down slides or roller coasters. I was too busy trying to survive. The thought of just jumping off the side of a mountain was horrifying to me. So, yeah, I did basically prefer the man-eating spiders.

"Think you can do this?" Elizabeth asks, lifting a brow in challenge.

Damn it, now I can't back down. "If you can do it, I can do it."

She climbs to the edge and swings her feet into the middle of the slide.

"Shouldn't someone else go first? Just in case?" I ask, heart racing.

She winks at me, then pushes herself off the edge. We hear her as she disappears into the distance, and her laugh-scream is just about the cutest thing I've ever heard in my life. And I didn't think many things were cute.

"Who's next?" Ax asks, grinning.

I force myself not to take a step back. I'm a dark fae. I can't let them know how much I *don't* want to go down that slide.

"Be my guest," I say, gesturing toward it.

So the bastard walks to the edge, sits down, and pushes off, just as fast as Elizabeth. Completely fearless. Like he's not going to be shooting down the side of a dangerous mountain, out of control.

I grumble. *These people are insane.*

Blade goes next, wincing as he sits, then hesitates, locks eyes with me, and pushes off.

Storm and I are left. He gestures for me to go.

I shake my head. "You go."

Suddenly, he snatches the keys from my hand and goes over the edge.

Fuck! My heart's in my throat as I jump off after him. My gaze is focused on the bastard who dared to betray us. To steal the keys. Now. When we were so close to the end of this nightmare.

The mountain flashes away around us, but my descent is slowed every time I start building to a dangerous speed by patches of grasses or moss, I wasn't sure which. I only know that the slide down isn't *as* awful as I'd imagined it.

When I get to the bottom, it's all moss, and I slow and slow until my feet hit the ground almost gently. Instantly, I leap to my feet and spot Storm. I'm on top of him, knocking him to the ground before he can run away. I stretch my powers out to end him, but he holds the keys out to me grinning.

"Gabriel!" Elizabeth shouts my name, and I hesitate.

"He stole the keys!" I say, reaching for his mind.

"I just wanted to give you more of an incentive to use the slide," he says, and there's humor in his voice.

I grab the keys and climb off of him, shaking. Elizabeth's arms are around me in an instant. She kisses my face over and over again until my heartbeat starts to calm, and I wrap myself around her, breathing in her scent, relaxing against my woman.

"Better?" Ax says, sounding far too smug.

But all I can do is nod.

Elizabeth moves between us, showering us with kisses and praise, and stops to check Blade's stomach wound. Her brows draw down, and she kisses him even harder, which tells me it's pretty damn bad. Luckily for the vampire-shifter, I knew he'd be fine. With time.

"We have the keys," I say.

She pauses and everyone looks at me.

"It's time to end this."

We just had to make the right choice.

Starting back through the foggy forest, I end the life of every creature that dares to get too close. I'm feeling tired. Weary. It seems to be more and more exhausting to kill our enemies. The last one that creeps up actually manages to leap out, but Ax cuts it in half with his blade. I'm thankful when we come to the end of the forest where the fog dissipates.

This challenge almost destroyed us. But through some miracle, we'd made it.

We'd won.

29

ELIZABETH

A s we step off the magic mountain and the fog
fades away, hands close around me. My sword
gets knocked away, and I'm dragged to the side.
As the world comes into focus, I feel the bite of a sword at
my throat. I shift slightly and realize the head demon, Draggos, is holding me, inching backward with me. The last of
his demons is at his side, and I'm getting further and further
from my men.

But my guys can see what's happening now, and the fury
in their faces makes my heart skip a beat.

"Give her back," Gabriel growls.

The demon shakes his head. "No, you will give us the
key, and we will give you back your woman unharmed. That
is our deal. Refuse us? We kill her."

"Why didn't you just get it yourself? Why stoop to this?"
Storm asks, his words a growl.

The demons exchange an amused look, and Draggos
says, "why do it ourselves when we can have *you* do it?"

I reach for my powers, gritting my teeth, aiming for the
demons, imagining them exploding all over this damned

place. But even though I can push through the dark, oily veil... nothing happens.

Is it that I can't see them? Is it that my powers are depleted? I didn't understand, but my heart starts to race, and the reality of our situation hits me like a bucket of cold water.

I could die now. Or all of us could die now.

The decision was easy.

Gabriel looks at me, and I give the slightest shake of my head. The fact that he hasn't killed them either means we're both too drained, or that it was the veil over our powers. But they can't give them the key now. Not after all we've been through.

"What's it going to be?" The demon hisses. "Your woman or the key?"

Gabriel doesn't hesitate. "The key."

"No!" I snap, my heart aching. If he gives the demon the key, we're all dead. "We made it to the end. Let them kill me. Get out yourselves!"

Even as I say the words, a cold resolve seems to come over my men. My chest aches because I know what that look means, and it makes my throat feel tight. I can't look away from them. My men have to know this is the right move. They have to know that dying with me is useless.

But their expressions say otherwise.

"You know we won't do that," Storm finally says.

Gabriel reaches forward, and my heart pounds. My men seem to be tense, waiting.

My dark fae presses something into his hand, and the demon steps back, grinning. I can't see if he gave him the wooden key, the gold key, or both, but I pray it was just the golden key. I might not know my father, but I knew he wanted me to live. If he said to go out the wooden door, that was the way to go.

The demon that holds me keeps inching back.

"We made a deal!" Gabriel shouts.

"We'll let her go. When we know the key fits!"

"That wasn't the deal!" Ax shouts.

I can hear the smile in the demon's voice. "The second I let her go, you're going to attack and kill us. She's our insurance."

My heart races and sweat beads at my forehead as we move backwards. I can't see where we're going, but I hope and pray it's to the golden door. Maybe, just maybe, if they step through it, we'll get a chance to try the other door.

I hear the demon stop.

I try to look behind us a little, but the sword slices into my neck, and I gasp, looking forward once more.

The sound of the key clicking in the door seems to radiate through the room.

"Because we're kind, we'll take your female with us," the demon hisses behind me.

With... them? Never. Never would I leave my men behind.

"No!" I say, the word wrenching from my lips. "I'm staying with my men."

I look at my men. Their hearts are in their eyes, and my hands curl into fists. These fools, how could they be willing to die for me, but not be willing to let me do the same?

"Take her with you," Storm says, and there's so much pain in his voice.

"If you take me, I'll kill you the instant I can," I promise, my teeth clenching together.

The demon laughs. My stomach tightens. And then, he pulls the sword from my throat and pushes me forward. I hit the ground hard, on my knees, and then turn to see the demons pushing open the golden door and stepping through.

My men race to my side.

"Let's go in while we can!" Ax shouts.

"No!" I scream.

Gabriel lifts me to my feet as if to carry me through the door.

I grab Ax's shirt, keeping him from stepping forward. "We have to go through the wooden door. Do you hear me? I know it's the right way. Trust me!"

They're all looking at me. Unsure.

So I say the one thing I know will work, and hope that my father was right. "I'm going through the wooden door, with or without you."

After a second, Storm says, "then we go through the wooden door."

Through the golden door, we can see the demons stepping through a field of flowers and trees. The light that shines down on them looks like the rays of the sun. My heart aches at the sight of it. *Is that truly freedom? Are we giving up everything just because of my trust in my father?*

Gabriel presses the wooden key into my hand. "We trust you."

We all walk toward the wooden door in the shadowy corner. A chill rolls down my spine and every hair on my body stands on end. I look behind me, and all my men look too. The bulbs around the golden door are flickering. My stomach sinks, but I keep going to the wooden door. Behind me, I hear the sound of the bulbs bursting.

I feel sick.

Someone was about to die.

Us? Them? I had no idea.

But no one speaks.

I stop in front of the door. My hand is sweaty as I push the key into the lock. Taking several deep breaths, I look at my men. Ax smiles. Blade nods. Storm lifts a brow, and Gabriel's eyes seem to worship me. Some of my fear fades away. They love me. They trust me with their lives. So I had to trust my gut too.

Looking back at the door, I turn the lock, and push the door open.

30

ELIZABETH

I n front of us is another dark hallway. Not a meadow of flowers. Not sunshine. Just a dark hallway lit by a few torches. That rush of anxiety returns, and for one minute I contemplate turning around and seeing if the key is still in the golden door. But then, I curl my hands into fists and start forward.

My guys follow closely behind me, and there's nothing but the sound of their breathing, and my heart beat. Twenty steps in, we all jump at a loud boom behind us. Spinning around, I see that the door has shut.

Truly, there's no going back now.

Gabriel takes my hand, and I'm surprised when Blade grabs my other hand. We keep going forward, but the tunnel seems to go on forever, slowly sloping up. There's nothing along the way. No doors. No windows. No other paths. Just the one tunnel forever leading up.

Hours past. My throat and legs ache.

I'm about to suggest we take a break when we round a corner and see a door at the end of the tunnel. The. End. Of. The. Tunnel. This was it. The lone wooden door could just be the same damn one we'd come through. All of this could be a trick. We could be like Storm, just being set up for the next big test.

We stop at the door. I look back at Storm and Ax, and they both squeeze my shoulders. Gabriel and Blade squeeze my hands. Then, I let go of their hands, reach forward, and turn the knob.

Like a dream, I pull it back and a blinding light washes over us. We shuffle forward, out of the darkness. The piercing light fades, and I blink as I stare at a fence.

Someone starts to slow clap, and it's like a damn nightmare. My gaze snaps to the sound, and the warden and his guards round the corner, their guns pointed at us.

Fucking déjà vu. This has to be a joke.

The warden's face widens into a smile. *Of course the bastard would smile at this.* "Very good. You escaped. Again."

"You fucking bastard!" Gabriel shouts.

"*Watch it,* dark fae. You might be able to kill me, but I promise you my guards will kill your little girlfriend in the same instant."

My shock fades replaced by anger. "What the fuck is wrong with you! *Another* test? *Another* game? We're people! Not your damn playthings!"

The warden's eyes flash with something unnamed. "Who said that any of this was a game? No, Elizabeth, this was not a game. This was not something for my amusement or entertainment. Far from it, actually."

"Then what is this?" I ask, the words cracking with rage.

He smiles. "You four... you're going to save the world."

31

ELIZABETH

We round the corner and spot a plastic bin outside of the stone walls of the building. Inside are what looks like the shredded remains of bodies. My gut clenches, and I look away, heart racing.

The warden catches my gaze and grins. "Those were your competitors, the demons. They chose the wrong door."

I feel sick. Not just because of the bodies, but because of how close we came to being them.

Silently, I thank my father. Maybe he hasn't been in my life much, but he sure as hell knew when to show up. And in a strange way, I think that's what makes a father.

"How did you know?" he asks, his voice cool.

I jerk and look back at the warden. "Know what?"

"Which door to go through? We watched all the competitions, and you were so confident that it was the right one. So confident that the bigger, stronger, prisoners believed you."

I hold his gaze. "Lucky guess."

"Oh?" his eyes narrow. "You have no idea how much I

want to pull you apart and find out what makes you tick. My... friends wanted your group to win. I wanted the demons to win. In the end, we threw in the doors to give a level of chance to the final competition. I never expected, that whatever you are, might help you figure it out."

"And you have no idea how much I want to kill you," Gabriel growls from behind me.

The warden laughs, and then his gaze goes to Storm. "So, wolf, how does it feel to be finally free? How does it feel to have finally picked the winning team?"

Storm's eyes narrow. "I have seen you die many times. It always makes me laugh."

The warden's eyes widen, and I swear he actually inches away from our group.

We approach a barbed wire fence. The same damn one that I'd come here through. The men with guns surround us, but none of them cuff us. None of them even speak. On the other side of the gate is a limo with darkly tinted windows. *Is that where we're heading?* I hardly thought prisoners got rides in limos.

"You said we were going to save the world," I say. "How?"

The warden tenses, then reaches into his pocket and draws out his cigarette, lighting it as we walk as if we're old friends having a chat. Slowly, he speaks, "I don't know. And even if I did, I wouldn't tell you. I'm just following orders."

Two guards open the door in the barbed wire fence as we approach. I can't read anything from their expressions, but our huge party pushes forward. Suddenly, the guards leap onto us. I feel the collar that goes around my throat and scream, but it's already too late. The guys are trying to fight, but they're already collared, and then one of the guards starts to shoot into the air.

We're breathing hard on the ground, the guards towering above us.

"Now your powers are bound." The warden grins, his dark eyes filled with cruelty.

"Fucking ass," Ax mumbles.

A guard kicks my shapeshifter like he's a Goddamn animal. I reach for my powers... and they're not there. My hands curl into fists, and I long to beat the shit out of every one of these assholes.

One day. I promise myself.

"Get into the limo," the warden growls, taking a long drag of his cigarette before puffing it out as he continues, "And if you do as they say, you might just live to see tomorrow."

My men all look at me. I know they're wondering if we should get into the car, fight, or run. I don't know the right answer. The car's the most unknown of the choices, but I doubt any of us would survive if we tried to fight or run.

"Okay," I say, nodding at my men.

Ax helps me to my feet, and then our dirty, tired group goes to the limo. A guard opens the door, and I climb in first, followed by my guys. We sit, and my gaze runs over the space. Near the front, several men in black suits sit together. I stiffen, recognizing the Enforcers's clothes.

My heart's in my throat, and it's hard to swallow.

The door closes behind us, sealing us in.

One of the Enforcers removes his glasses, and suddenly I'm face-to-face with the man who put me here in the first place. The Enforcer who said I'd killed the guards. The man who had me torchered for information.

"What the fuck do you want?"

His eyes narrow. "Of course, it had to be *you*."

"*What* had to be me?"

He glares, not answering me

"Do you know each other?" Ax asks, and there's a protective note to his voice.

The Enforcer glares. "I wanted the best of the best, and I got *you*."

"Fuck you!"I say, and I jump out of my seat.

My nails dig into his cheek, and then he punches me in the face. I snap back and my men go wild.

The guards leap into action, shoving and punching, and then the man screams, "Stop if you want to fucking live!"

Everyone stops. My men climb back from the Enforcers and gather around me, pulling me onto the seat between Gabriel and Storm. And as much as I don't want to start another fight, I can't seem to control my anger.

I'm breathing hard. "You threw me in here. You stole my life!"

His gaze meets mine. "Have you ever stopped to think we're not the bad guys here?"

"No!"

"Then you're a fool!"

"Fuck you!" Ax shouts, and I look at him to see blood rolling down from a cut in his cheek.

Storm speaks more softly. "Yes, because good men punch women and falsely imprison innocents."

The man wipes at the bloody claw marks on his face from my nails. "Sometimes you have to crack a few eggs to make an omelet."

"And what, we're the *eggs*?"

He stares at me for a long minute before speaking. "We needed the best of the best for a... project. We only get one shot at this, and the warden promised to deliver the strongest group of prisoners in all his control. He assures us... you are them."

None of us speak. We just wait.

"We have a task for you. A task, as I said, that you get one shot at. If you lose, our world will change forever. Evil will seep into every inch of it and destroy supernaturals and humanity alike... everything in this world that's precious."

"And why should we care?" Gabriel asks, glaring.

The man leans forward and steeples his hands. "Because, should you survive this task, we will erase your records. We will pay you a king's ransom in money, and we will release you. You will live the rest of your lives as free people. More than free people, rich, powerful people."

"And what if we don't want this deal of yours?" Blade asks, his expression blanks.

The man smiles. "Then we kill all of you and start over in our quest to find adequate prisoners."

Everyone looks at me.

My hands curl into fists. "How do we know you won't betray us?"

He looks irritated. "I've been told to make it a blood promise. A promise that cannot be broken."

I think of my mom. I think of the human world I came from. No, I didn't trust this guy, but if what he's telling us is true, then I needed to do whatever I could to keep the evil I've seen from destroying the beautiful things in this world.

I look at my men.

"It's up to you," Gabriel whispers. "You know we'll follow you to hell and back."

They already had.

I look at Storm and Blade. I can practically feel our shifter sides reaching for me, claiming me as theirs.

And then my gaze falls onto Ax. For a minute something sinister crosses his face, and I'm surprised when I shiver. Something was happening with him. I needed to get him away from the death and cruelty. I needed to give him a happy life.

This might be our only chance at that.

A second later, his expression grows confused, and he looks at me. Waiting for my answer.

Damn it. My choice was already made.

"Okay,' I say. "We'll do it."

He looks at his guards and nods. Their guns lift. and I'm staring at the end of a barrel when I hear the explosion of the trigger.

Then, everything goes black.

Dɪᴅ you enjoy the second book in the Paranormal Prison shared world? If so, preorder your copy of book three, Chosen Warriors.

WELCOME TO NIGHTMARE PENITENTIARY

PARANORMAL
PRISON

ALSO BY LACEY CARTER ANDERSEN

Monsters and Gargoyles

Medusa's Destiny *audiobook*

Keto's Tale

Celaeno's Fate

Cerberus Unleashed

Lamia's Blood

Shade's Secret

Hecate's Spell

Shorts: Their Own Sanctuary

Shorts: Their Miracle Pregnancy

Dark Supernaturals

Wraith Captive

Marked Immortals

Wicked Reform School/House of Berserkers

Untamed: Wicked Reform School

Unknown: House of Berserkers

Royal Fae Academy

Revere (A Short Prequel)

Ravage

Ruin

Reign

Her Alien Mates

Collection: Her Alien Romance

Steamy Tales of Warriors and Rebels

Gladiators

The Dragon Shifters' Last Hope

Claimed by Her Harem

Treasured by Her Harem

Collection: Magic in her Harem

Harem of the Shifter Queen

Sultry Fire

Sinful Ice

Saucy Mist

Collection: Power in her Kiss

Standalones

Worthy (A Villainously Romantic Retelling)

Beauty with a Bite

Shifters and Alphas

Collections

Monsters, Gods, Witches, Oh My!

Wings, Horns, and Shifters

ABOUT THE AUTHOR

Lacey Carter Andersen loves reading, writing, and drinking excessive amounts of coffee. She spends her days taking care of her husband, three kids, and three cats. But at night, everything changes! Her imagination runs wild with strong-willed characters, unique worlds, and exciting plots that she enthusiastically puts into stories.

Lacey has dozens of tales: science fiction romances, paranormal romances, short romances, reverse harem romances, and more. So, please feel free to dive into any of her worlds; she loves to have the company!

And you're welcome to reach out to her; she really enjoys hearing from her readers.

You can find her at:

Email: laceycarterandersen@gmail.com

Mailing List: https://www.subscribepage.com/laceycarterandersen

Website: www.laceycarterandersen.wordpress.com/

Facebook Page: www.facebook.com/Lacey-Carter-Andersen-1940678949483316/

Printed in Great Britain
by Amazon